"We're going to go out right now and get our own sampling of what women are interested in."

A dimple dented Cal's cheek as he smiled. "Though if you want to fill one of these surveys out, you're welcome to."

Kit shot him a look. "No, thanks."

"I don't think I will either, though I do appreciate your interest in me."

"I'm not interested in you!" she returned too fast. "Where do we start?"

"Central Park, of course. I bet there are a bunch of Little League-type games going on. We'll probably find hundreds of women like you."

"Excuse me, Mr. Panagos," Kit said, feigning insult. "But there are *no* women like me."

Cal stopped and looked over at her with a smile. "No, I don't think there are."

Dear Reader,

If you're eagerly anticipating holiday gifts we can start you off on the right foot, with six compelling reads by authors established and new. Consider it a somewhat early Christmas, Chanukah or Kwanzaa present!

The gifting begins with another in *USA TODAY* bestselling author Susan Mallery's DESERT ROGUES series. In *The Sheik and the Virgin Secretary* a spurned assistant decides the only way to get over a soured romance is to start a new one—with her prince of a boss (literally). Crystal Green offers the last installment of MOST LIKELY TO… with *Past Imperfect*, in which we finally learn the identity of the secret benefactor—as well as Rachel James's parentage. Could the two be linked? In *Under the Mistletoe*, Kristin Hardy's next HOLIDAY HEARTS offering, a by-the-book numbers cruncher is determined to liquidate a grand New England hotel…until she meets the handsome hotel manager determined to restore it to its glory days—and capture her heart in the process! Don't miss *Her Special Charm*, next up in Marie Ferrarella's miniseries THE CAMEO. This time the finder of the necklace is a gruff New York police detective—surely he can't be destined to find love with its Southern belle of an owner, can he? In *Diary of a Domestic Goddess* by Elizabeth Harbison, a woman who is close to losing her job, her dream house and her livelihood finds she might be able to keep all three—*if* she can get close to her hotshot new boss who's annoyingly irresistible. And please welcome brand-new author Loralee Lillibridge—her debut book, *Accidental Hero*, features a bad boy come home, this time with scars, an apology—and a determination to win back the woman he left behind!

So celebrate! We wish all the best of everything this holiday season and in the New Year to come.

Happy reading,

Gail Chasan
Senior Editor

Please address questions and book requests to:
Silhouette Reader Service
U.S.: 3010 Walden Ave., P.O. Box 1325, Buffalo, NY 14269
Canadian: P.O. Box 609, Fort Erie, Ont. L2A 5X3

DIARY OF A
DOMESTIC GODDESS

ELIZABETH HARBISON

Silhouette

SPECIAL EDITION®

Published by Silhouette Books

America's Publisher of Contemporary Romance

SILHOUETTE BOOKS

ISBN 0-373-24727-3

DIARY OF A DOMESTIC GODDESS

Visit Silhouette Books at www.eHarlequin.com

Printed in U.S.A.

Books by Elizabeth Harbison

Silhouette Special Edition

Drive Me Wild #1476
Midnight Cravings #1539
How To Get Your Man #1685
Diary of a Domestic Goddess #1727

Silhouette Romance

A Groom for Maggie #1239
Wife Without a Past #1258
Two Brothers and a Bride #1286
True Love Ranch #1323
*Emma and the Earl #1410
*Plain Jane Marries the Boss #1416
*Annie and the Prince #1423
*His Secret Heir #1528
A Pregnant Proposal #1553
Princess Takes a Holiday #1643
The Secret Princess #1713
Taming of the Two #1790

*Cinderella Brides

Silhouette Books

Lone Star Country Club
Mission Creek Mother-To-Be

ELIZABETH HARBISON

has been an avid reader for as long as she can remember. After authoring three cookbooks, Elizabeth turned her hand to writing romances and hasn't looked back. Her second book for Silhouette Romance, *Wife Without a Past,* was a 1998 finalist for the Romance Writers of America's prestigious RITA® Award in the "Best Traditional Romance" category.

Elizabeth lives in Maryland with her husband, John, daughter Mary Paige, and son, Jack, as well as two dogs, Bailey and Zuzu. She loves to hear from readers, and you can write to her c/o Box 1636, Germantown, MD 20875.

Dedicated to Greg Cunliffe, the best friend I ever had,
in loving memory.

And to Yolande Cunliffe and Jane Cunliffe Aylor,
with heartfelt thanks for your friendship in the difficult
times we've shared and in the brighter times yet to come.

Chapter One

Edith's Diary
Home Life *Magazine*
October 2005 issue

As the days grow shorter and the air carries the crisp bite of autumn, my thoughts turn to cool red apples, amber sunlight and ghosts and goblins with flashlights wandering the narrow country lane of our home in the Virginia hills. Steve has picked a pumpkin from the sunny patch on the hill and is in the kitchen right now sketching out an elaborate jack-o'-lantern using the stencil pattern on page twenty-two. Little Johnny is standing by, watching with fascination. Soon he'll come in to help me make his pirate costume. That's right, we're making it. No more hot plastic masks that smell like glue, no nylon costumes that fall apart halfway through your little one's candy pilgrimage. Everything you need to make a wonderful and memorable Halloween costume is probably already in your house.

"Mommy!"
"Just a minute."

For the pirate costume, gather a red bandanna, black sweatpants, long white sweat socks, aluminum foil, a woman's long-sleeved blouse, some gold craft paint and a plastic shower curtain ring for the pirate's earring—

"Mom*my!*"
Kit Macy stopped typing and pushed her laptop back on the ancient Formica kitchen table with exaggerated patience. Then she turned to the four-year-old who was still tugging on her sleeve. "Are you on fire?"

"No—"

"Are you bleeding?"

"No, but—"

She lowered her chin. "Are you supposed to interrupt me when I'm working?"

Johnny pressed his lips together and glanced at the kitchen doorway behind him before saying, "No."

Big, guilty kid eyes. They got to her every time. Kit smiled and ruffled his hair. "Look, I know you're hot and bored. Just let me finish and we can go to the pool, okay? Maybe Mr. Finnegan can fix the air conditioner while we're gone." It was July, and the mugginess of the New Jersey summer had already hit them full force. The fan Kit had propped in the corner of the small apartment kitchen sputtered ominously, and she glanced at it. "Before that thing dies, too, and we melt." One more month and she would be closing on her own house. A house with central air-conditioning and a community pool.

Sometimes it was the only thought that kept her going.

Johnny gave a distracted nod. "Okay, but Mommy?"

She sighed. "Yes?"

"Um, Mommy?"

"Johnny, *what?*"

"Steve has something stuck on his nose."

It took a moment for her to rewind and replay the mental tape. "What is it?"

He squirmed visibly around the question. "He wouldn't come with me to show you."

Two nights ago Johnny had smeared peanut butter on Steve's nose because it was "so funny to watch him try and lick it off." A quick calculation told Kit that if Steve wasn't in the kitchen—and he wasn't—it was likely that he was in the TV room with her new sofa. Her new twelve-hundred-dollar Open Space sofa with the custom vine-patterned upholstery. That and peanut butter would make for an ugly combination. Actually anything and peanut butter made for an ugly combination.

She jumped up. "Where is he?"

"In my room," Johnny admitted, his voice small behind her as she dashed out of the kitchen.

She rounded the corner to the small, dark hallway and heard repeated sneezes behind Johnny's closed bedroom door. "You're not supposed to lock him in there, baby, you know that."

"I know," Johnny answered, drawing each syllable out guiltily.

Kit pushed the door open and saw Steve, the black Labrador mutt, lying on the floor, sneezing and growling and trying to wrestle something off his nose.

"Damn." She dropped to the floor and tried to calm the squirming dog down enough to remove the shower curtain ring she'd gotten out of the bathroom to make an earring for the stupid pirate costume. "Damn, damn, damn."

"You said a bad thing!"

"You're right." She pried the ring open and pulled it off the dog's nose, trying to resist saying another stream of "bad things." "You know you're not supposed to put people things on Steve. I've told you that like a hundred times already."

"That's not a people thing," Johnny said, his voice stern with four-year-old condescension. "It's a *bathroom* thing."

"Today it's a people thing." Arguing with him was like arguing with a slick Jersey lawyer. He always came up with some loophole she hadn't previously covered. Last week, in the late-night emergency pediatric clinic, it was that she'd never actually *said* not to put the wheels from his Matchbox cars into his ears. Now she looked at him pointedly. "But, for the record, keep bathroom things away from Steve, too." She examined the plastic ring. If it had managed to squeeze that tightly on Steve's nose, it probably wouldn't be all that good for a toddler's ear. Frankly it had struck her as a stupid idea when the woman from the local playgroup had mentioned it in the first place. Now she'd have to come up with an alternative before her deadline.

"What's it for anyway?" Johnny asked, taking the ring from her and immediately getting it stuck on his fingertip. He barely had time to whip up a good whine before Kit reached over and pulled it off with a snap.

"It's supposed to be for your costume."

He looked skeptical. No, afraid. "I don't like it."

"Neither does Steve." Upon hearing his name, the dog pushed his wet nose against her hand and she patted his head.

"I don't like pirates."

"You don't have to."

"I don't like boats," Johnny went on, clearly covering all pirate bases so that she wouldn't try to convince him to be, say, a superhero pirate. "And I don't like earrings. I don't like them at *all*."

Sometimes it felt as if he was plucking at her nerves as though they were strings on an out-of-tune ukulele. "Look, buddy, you don't *need* to like pirates. You don't need to wear the costume on Halloween. All you need to do is be a kid long enough for me to make sure these homemade costumes work so I can print them in my column."

Though he was only four, Johnny had long since understood that all the quirky domestic things his mother worked on were part of her job as "Edith Chamberlain," *Home Life* magazine's monthly "Edith's Diary" columnist. She'd been the managing editor of the magazine for five years now, but she'd taken over writing the column two and a half years ago when the real Edith Chamberlain—who had established the column forty years ago—had passed away.

"I don't want to be a princess, either," Johnny said in a small, husky voice. He'd been saying it ever since she'd taken him to the craft store to get the glitter for the princess costume she was also detailing in her article.

Kit gave the dog one last pat, then stood up. "Yeah, well, you're just trying the costume on for me, then we'll take it off really fast, okay?"

His voice went glum. "Okay."

She looked at her watch. "In fact, we should do it now because your dad's gonna come pick you up when he gets off work in an hour."

"You said we could go to the pool!"

"We will. We'll try the costume on really quick, then we'll go to the pool and watch for him from there. Deal?"

"Okay." He was already busy peeling off his sweaty Batman T-shirt and the pull-up diapers her mother kept telling her he was too old for.

"Just put him in regular underpants," Kit's mother would say. "If he messes them up, he'll get uncomfortable in a hurry."

"He doesn't seem to have a problem with walking around in a poopie pull-up," Kit pointed out every time. "How much difference will it make if it's underpants instead? It would just make more work for me."

But Kit's mother was never wrong, even when she was patently incorrect. She just clicked her tongue against her teeth, shook her head knowingly and said, "You coddle that child too much."

It wasn't a surprising sentiment from her mother, she realized, considering the fact that Kit had done more to raise her two younger sisters than her working mom had, but it still made her feel bad.

"Got it!" Johnny called in a singsong voice. Kit hadn't even realized he'd left the room, but he was walking back in with the pale blue princess dunce cap—she made a mental note to find out what the real name for it was before printing the column—perched on his head at a rakish angle. He dragged the satiny dress—made entirely with a tank dress from Target and cheap, shiny polyester fabric ironed on with stitching tape—behind him. The glitter they'd stuck on with glue left a vaguely Disney-like trail behind him.

She had to hand it to him, he really was a good sport.

Kit went to him. "Put your arms up." He did, and she slid the dress over his head. She had to admit it looked pretty good. Perhaps a little like a trailer-park prom dress, but that was what Halloween was *supposed* to look like. "How does it feel?" she asked. "Comfortable? Move around a little bit."

He struck a superhero pose, then ran across the floor and back again, feet stomping hard on the wood floor. Thank goodness it was just the Finnegans living beneath them, since they were both all but deaf. When he got back he nodded his approval. "It's good."

"I wonder if it will hold together," she said, tugging gently at the hem. She was alarmed to see that the stitching tape was starting to pull apart when there was a knock at the door. "Wait there," she instructed Johnny, pressing the hem together before getting up. "Don't move."

He stood still and she admired the costume one more time, hoping she might be able to improvise a quick fix. Maybe a glue gun? She was so distracted by the thought that when she opened the door and saw her ex-husband, it took a moment to compute. Why wasn't he at work?

"Rick."

"Daddy!" Johnny cried from across the room.

"Hey, bud."

Johnny ran to Rick, arms outspread, dress coming apart more with every step. He threw himself into Rick's arms, distributing pale blue glitter all over Rick's Grateful Dead T-shirt.

Rick looked at his son. "What've *you* got on?"

Johnny flashed his mother a look of dramatic disapproval. "A princess costume."

Rick looked over Johnny's shoulder at Kit. "The column again?"

Kit nodded.

"They really ought to pay you extra for doing that. Put some money aside for therapy." Rick laughed.

"Very funny. You're early."

"I know, I know, but I borrowed a car from my neighbor and I have to get it back to her by six." Rick was six years younger than Kit, and once upon a time she had been enamored by his long-haired starving-artist persona. Now she was just weary of it.

"What happened to your company car?" she asked, dreading the answer even before the words were out of her mouth. He didn't lose his job. Please, God, don't let him say he lost his job.

Rick clicked his tongue against his teeth and let out a long *aah* breath. "I'm just not a corporate drone." He set Johnny down. "I gave it a try—and I really appreciate your helping me get me the job and all—but it just wasn't me." He was unfazed by the withering look she was giving him. "The good news is, I got a gig painting a mural on the side of that old brick building on Maryland Avenue and Dobrey Street."

"Does it pay?"

He tipped a flattened hand from side to side. "But the exposure is great. The theme is Indonesian history." He nodded, as if that would make Kit feel all better about her son's father's complete lack of financial prospects.

Kit just looked at him. "Indonesian history."

"What's that?" Johnny asked.

"Excellent question, my friend." Rick ruffled Johnny's hair. "We'll look it up this weekend."

"You have to *look it up?*" Kit repeated incredulously. "You got this job without even knowing *anything* about it?"

Rick just smiled and said to Johnny, "Change your clothes—we have to go."

"Okay. I'll be right back!"

When Johnny was gone, Rick looked at Kit with pity. "Rough week?"

"What?"

"You look like hell. And you've got that past-deadline-temper thing going. You work too much."

She frowned. "I have to. I'm trying to buy a house for *our* son. And it will be a lot easier if you keep up your support payments, such as they are."

He waved her concerns away. "Don't worry about it."

It was good advice, because worrying about Rick's lack of prospects had never made one whit of difference anyway. "So. Got big plans for the weekend? Besides studying Indonesian history, I mean."

"Thought I might take him into the city to see the Modigliani exhibit at MOMA."

"That would be good." Better Rick than Kit, she figured. It wouldn't hurt Johnny to be exposed to modern art, and God knew Kit didn't want to do it. Modigliani gave her a headache. She didn't like taking liberties with proportion. She was more of a Vermeer girl herself.

It wasn't a bad metaphor for her life with Rick.

"Then again, we might stay in and watch *Time Bandits*."

"Again?"

"Hey, it's a classic."

She couldn't help but laugh. She'd known what she was getting into when she'd married him, and now, when he was consistently what she expected, she could hardly call foul on him for it. At least he loved his son and took good care of him when it was his weekend.

Johnny pounded back in the room. The dress was gone and he was in a Batman shirt—inside out—and shorts. He hauled his overstuffed Buzz Lightyear suitcase across the floor noisily. Buzz himself, the beat-up three-pound toy that could double as a weapon in the event of a burglary, was sticking out of the top.

"Ready to go, Buzz?" Rick asked, reminding Kit why she had loved him once. He was really good with Johnny, there was no denying it.

"Yup, he's ready." Johnny pointed to the obvious projection from his bag.

Kit knelt by the boy and gave him a tight hug. "You have a good time with Daddy, okay?"

"Okay, Mommy."

She drew back and touched his nose. "I'll miss you."

"I'll miss you too. 'Bye!"

"'Bye, baby." She stood up.

"Relax a little," Rick said to her. "These sixty-hour weeks are too much. You need to just *be* sometimes, you know?"

And that, she realized all at once, was why she'd married him. That mellowness, that hippie-without-the-drugs peacefulness. That was why she'd married him.

And why the marriage had failed.

Because no matter how much she wanted to be that easygoing, mellow, pass-the-nachos person, she was always going to be the *uh-oh* woman.

Thank God Johnny had Rick around to balance that out.

"Yes," she agreed. "I need to *be* employed." She smiled. "But don't worry about me—I've got the whole weekend to eat bonbons and listen to Frank Sinatra on the CD player."

"Give it a try," Rick said with a smile. "Couldn't hurt." He looked down at Johnny. "Let's go. The car's about to turn into a pumpkin." He put his hand lightly on the back of Johnny's blond head and guided him into the hallway.

For a moment she watched Johnny's slight body walking away, his pipe-cleaner arm raised to hold his father's hand, then stepped back into her apartment. The door closed with a light click behind her. She still heard their footsteps—Rick's heavy plodding and the tap of Johnny's run—disappear like music at the end of a song. When they were gone and she knew she was safely alone, she smiled. The weekend was hers. She didn't have to make a single vegetable if she didn't want to. In fact, she could eat Cap'n Crunch over the sink for two nights in a row if that's what she wanted.

She had forty-eight hours to unwind the stress

that had wound her up all week and she had to start right away.

She got the Cap'n Crunch out.

Chapter Two

"The thing is, I don't think doctors actually give babies opium for teething anymore." Kit leaned her elbows on her desk and listened to the old medical columnist's patronizing response over the telephone line before responding, "I know it's called paregoric, but it's *opium*." And four years ago she would have given her right arm to have some for her screaming baby, but still. Come on. It was a narcotic. "How about you just try describing more homemade remedies, like teething rings, freezing a sock, that kind of thing…." She listened on the line again. "A *sock*. Like, for your feet. You soak it in water, then freeze it and…" She sighed. "Never mind. Just go ahead and finish your column."

She would edit it later.

Home Life magazine had been around for a hundred and twenty-five years, and Kit was willing to bet Orville Pippin had been writing his "Ask the Doctor" column for at least half that time. She would also bet his exploration of modern medicine stopped with whatever the Stenberg School of Medicine class of '38 had taken away under their graduation caps.

Kit had only been the managing editor of the magazine for five years, but in that time she'd researched and written more of his columns than he himself had, thanks to all of the outdated advice he had a tendency to dole out. She had a hotline to her own pediatrician's office to double-check just this kind of thing.

Opium.

Jeez.

"Hey, Kit!" Lucy, a young editorial assistant, barked from the hallway. "Phone, line two. Johnny's babysitter again."

Kit glanced at the clock. Two fifty-five. Damn. Five minutes ago it had been noon and even *then* she hadn't had enough time to finish everything she had to do today. She closed her eyes and counted to five. If she didn't pick up the phone, they couldn't tell her to come pick him up early again. It wasn't as if they'd put him out on the sidewalk.

She waited just a beat longer, then picked up the receiver. "This is Kit Macy."

"Ms. Macy." It was the director, Ellen Phillips. She always pronounced *Ms.* as if it contained twenty-two z's. "We seem to have a problem."

"Oh?"

"Yes, Johnny has been fighting with Kyle again." Big surprise. It was like saying Churchill and Hitler had had another disagreement. "It seems both of them wanted to ride the fire engine, but Johnny refused to let Kyle have a turn."

Kyle was a bully. Easily two years older than Johnny and at least twenty pounds heavier, the kid picked on Johnny every single day. One would have thought the facility administrator might have taken the older, bigger child to task, but she never did. Kyle's parents were a whole lot richer than Kit, and if Mizzzzzzz Phillips had to alienate either boy's parents, it was going to be Johnny's every time.

And it was.

Kit took a short breath. "Ellen, look, can't you please just separate them for the rest of the day?" She looked at the clock. Three o'clock. "It's only another two hours or so, and I have a million things I have to get done."

"I'm trying to do my job, too, Ms. Macy, but that's difficult to do with these hellions creating chaos for me."

Hellions. Man, she'd hissed it like a curse. "Well, maybe Kyle's parents can pick him up this time."

The phone line seemed to crackle with the chill of her response. "But you are in the building next door to ours. I would hate to ask Mr. Cherkins to come all the way downtown when you're right here."

Yes. Yes, she was *right here.* And that was the only reason she still had Johnny in the Petite Care Center. She was seriously thinking it wasn't worth it.

If Johnny hadn't been caught in the middle of this, Kit's response would have been different, but she didn't want to instigate an argument only to have Ellen take it out on the boy.

She looked at the clock on her desk. Three-oh-three. She sighed heavily. "I'll be right there."

"*He* wouldn't let *me* ride."

"I believe you." Kit toted Johnny along the sidewalk toward the old building that had served as *Home Life*'s headquarters since 1948. "But I've told you before to avoid that kid. If he's playing with something, you have to find something else to play with. If he's not near you, he can't fight with you."

"But I was there first!" Johnny's voice rang with the injustice of it. Obviously he'd had to explain this to Ellen, too, because his face crinkled the way it always did when he was truly frustrated.

"Then you should have walked away." Kit heard her own advice and stopped. To hell with hurrying back to work. This was more important.

She knelt down in front of her son on the grungy sidewalk, holding his slight shoulders in her hands. "I take it back, Johnny. You shouldn't have. You can't walk away every time a bully tries to take something from you. You did the right thing. I'm glad you stood up for yourself."

A dent formed in the perfectly smooth skin over his brow. "You are?" His blue eyes went dark with confusion. "But you just said—"

"I know, baby. But I was wrong. It's *easier* to walk away from bullies sometimes, but it's not always *right*." She pulled him close for a hug, reveling in the soft, soapy smell of his skin and hair. She kissed the cottony-soft blond head and drew back. "Okay?"

"I don't want to go back there."

It broke her heart. He was there for her convenience, not because it was best for him. There was no pretending otherwise. *She* was best for him. And since she couldn't be there all the time, she was going to have to find something else. Something that wasn't Mizzzzzzz Phillips. "Remember how I told you I was going to try and put you in that Montessori school near our new house?"

"School?" His eyes lit up. He was enamored with the idea of school in the way only a person who had never been could be.

She nodded, but fear surged in her heart rather than the hope she saw in his. What if it didn't work out? It didn't bear thinking about. "Well, the application came in the mail today and I'm going to send it back to them this afternoon. Well, tomorrow afternoon." After she was paid. The seventy-five-dollar application fee was nonnegotiable.

She knew because she'd tried to negotiate it.

"My new school," he said with a small nod and the kind of smile that made her determine right there and then that she'd get him into the school even if she had to rob a bank to do it. "And Kyle Cherkins won't be there, right?"

"No, he won't." She stood up again and took his little warm hand, leading him into the office. "Okay. Here we are. You know the drill. Sit quietly and color. No talking, no running, no interrupting me when I'm on the phone and no asking why Miss Pratt's ankles are so wrinkly. Got it?"

"I know, I know."

* * *

"Mommy! Mommy, Mommy." Tap, tap, tap on her arm. "Look, Mommy."

Kit held her hand over the mouthpiece of the phone and shot Johnny a *shut up* look. She returned to her call. "So you're saying you lost *all* of the documentation?"

The bank official on the other end of the line cleared his throat. "Your former loan officer left in something of a hurry. We don't know exactly where she put all the files she was working on. It's caused quite a backup, I must say."

Kit's heart lodged in her throat. "I'm not going to lose my interest rate, am I?"

"I sincerely hope not."

Kit's stomach dropped. "Wait. *Sincerely hope not* isn't good enough. I need to know." Or what? Or she'd go to another company? Although her credit was good, there were a few tiny glitches—a forgotten department store credit card that she'd once been thirty-one days late in paying, a collection effort on the part of *Big Jugs* magazine for a subscription she'd never ordered—that she'd had to clear with Best State Mortgage. She did *not* want to start the process over again.

"We'll do our best, Ms. Macy. If you could just get your bank statements, tax forms, W-2's and employer's statement to us, we'll get right on it."

"Employer's statement?" Unbelievable. They

needed something new every single time she talked to them.

"Just something stating your year-to-date earnings and projected income."

"Okay." She glanced at Johnny. Maybe it was a good thing she'd already gotten him, because now she was going to have to stay after and hope the editor, Ebbit, had time to write something up. "Anything else?"

"It's all on the checklist."

There was a beep on the line. The phone said it was in-house. Ebbit himself. "Okay, Mr. Black, I have copies of everything else, so I'll just overnight them to you again."

"No need to hurry."

"No need to hurry?" Her voice leaped toward hysteria. "I'm supposed to close on the house in twenty-eight days."

There was a nerve-racking pause.

Then the sound of papers shuffling on the other end of the line. "I'm sorry, did you say twenty-eight days? I have you down for September."

Johnny tapped Kit's arm and she pulled it away, turning her office chair around. "No, it's this month. July 30." It was all she could do to stay calm. If this stupid company prevented her from getting her house because one person screwed up, she'd—

"I'll make a note of it," the loan officer said noncommittally.

Kit's phone beeped again.

She thought her head might explode.

"All right. I have to take this call, Mr. Black, so I'll just collect the information and you'll have it in the morning." She clicked over to the other line.

"We have an urgent meeting this afternoon at five," Ebbit Markham told her.

"Okay." She glanced at Johnny. There was going to have to be some serious bribery involved in trying to keep him sitting quietly in her office during an editorial meeting. "Actually I'm glad you're staying a little late because I need you to give me a written statement that I work here."

Silence.

"Ebbit?"

"Why do you need that?"

She tapped her pen on the desk. "It's not a big deal. The mortgage company just wants proof that I'm employed." She gave a casual laugh. "You know how it is—they don't want to lend you money until you can completely prove you don't need it."

Again nothing.

"Oh! Yes, yes, well…" What was with him? He sounded as if she'd shocked him out of sleep or something. "I'll just, uh, I'll see you at five."

"Okay." She hung up the phone thoughtfully.

"Mommy." Johnny tapped her again. "Are you off the phone now? Look at my picture." He produced her May bank statement, replete with indelible ink scribbles. "It's our new house. Do you like it?"

"Yeah, honey, that's nice," she said, distracted.

Johnny tugged on her sleeve. "You didn't look at it. You have to *look* at it!"

She looked.

Oh, no. Oh. No. No, no, no. The bank statement. All those numbers.

In her mind's eye she saw herself spending the evening with a bottle of Wite-Out, removing every line he'd added. And even then she ran the risk of it looking as if she'd somehow doctored her books.

But Johnny looked so proud, so pleased with his work, that she couldn't bear to let out the anger that bubbled in her chest. "It's good," she said in a tight voice. "But, honey, next time ask me for paper, okay? Don't write on something that already has writing on it. That's *really important,* got it?"

"You don't like it?"

She took a long breath. "Yes, I do, it's just…" She sighed. "It's just great." She produced a pile of paper from her printer tray, looked at it and added a few more sheets. "Here. Do some more. I've got to go in the room next door for a meeting in a little while, and you're going to stay here, so why don't you draw all your very best friends for me. If you run out of paper, get more from there, okay?" She pointed to the printer tray.

He barely glanced at it, said, "'Kay," and set about drawing immediately.

She looked at her clock again.

It was four-forty.

Kit always thought that if Samantha Stevens had twitched her nose and turned an old basset hound into a man, she'd have ended up with Ebbit Markham. Today he looked even more basset houndish than usual, his face drawn and white.

The staff of *Home Life* was collected in the conference room. Ebbit's lifelong secretary, Miss Pratt—no one was sure of her first name—was handing out coffee in foam cups, her shaking hands sloshing the hot liquid onto laps, shirts and the floor.

"What's going on?" Kit asked her friend Joanna Sadler, aka Joe Sadler, Mr. Fix-It, another monthly columnist as well as the permissions editor.

"Don't freak" was Joanna's first response.

Kit quirked her mouth into a smile, belying the nervous tremor in her stomach. "Okay, now that I know it's freakworthy, *what's going on?*"

"I think the magazine's been sold."

"What?"

"It's just what I heard. I could be wrong."

How could this happen without her knowing something was up in advance? "Who bought it?"

Joanna shrugged. "Some idiot who wants a century-old monthly that's hopelessly outdated and losing readers by the score every day, I guess."

It was a fair assessment, Kit knew. The once venerable publication had become so desperate for readers that it offered subscriptions for the cost of postage. Every time she'd suggested to Ebbit that maybe they should become a little more contemporary, he gave her a lecture on tradition.

Lucy came up next to Kit, her small, tanned face tight with worry. "They sold the magazine? What's going to happen to us?"

"Hang on—we don't know anything yet," Kit said, trying to inject reason. "As far as we know, this is just a regular editorial meeting."

In her gut she knew it wasn't.

The door opened and a tall, slick-looking man with dark hair, light eyes, a square jaw and a suit that probably cost almost as much as her monthly salary walked in.

Everyone made their way to their seats around the conference table and turned to face Ebbit at the head of the table like obedient schoolchildren.

He stood behind his chair rather than sitting down. "As you all know," he began, clutching and unclutching the back of the chair with gnarled hands. "I have been working for *Home Life* for over fifty years. I began in the mail room and worked my way slowly but surely to where I am now." He glanced at the man with him. "Or, that is, where I was until today."

This was not good.

Ebbit mustered a smile. "*Home Life* has been sold, along with her sister publications, to the Monahan Group. If the name sounds familiar to you, it's because they own and operate such publications as *Sports World, Kidz* and *Celeb Dish* magazines." He looked at the man with him. "With the new management comes a new direction for all of us. As of today, I am entering into that wonderful state called *retirement.*" His voice wavered over the word retirement. "I plan to do a lot of fishing and gardening and generally get on Connie's nerves."

There was a small wave of polite laughter in the room.

"Anyhoo," Ebbit said in his wrapping-it-up voice, "this is Cal Panagos." He gestured toward the man. "Cal is the former editor of *Sports World.* Now he's the new executive editor of *Home Life.*"

Ebbit stepped aside, and Cal Panagos stepped behind the chair as if it was a grand podium. "Thanks for the welcome," he said, giving Ebbit a stiff but technically courteous nod. His bearing was positively regal. His looks were as strikingly sultry as one of the Calvin Klein underwear models who routinely looked over Times Square with long-lashed bedroom eyes. But it was his air of confidence that struck Kit the most.

He set his expensive-looking leather briefcase on the table and opened it up. "I know this is a surprise to many of you."

Kit's stomach turned over. Her heart pounded as if a boxer was caught in her rib cage. This couldn't be happening. Yet it was.

She was losing her house.

Cal continued. "Personally I'm excited about the challenge this presents."

Kit noticed he tensed his jaw for a moment. It was a gesture that hardened the planes of his face and made him look even more manly.

"My plan is to start this magazine over from the ground up, and I'm bringing in my own people for the task, so…" His expensively clad shoulders rose a fraction of an inch, then dropped. "I thank you for your years of service to *Home Life* and, if you'll make your way to Ebbit's former office, you'll find your severance packages waiting for you."

The room responded with silence. No gasps, no objections.

"I believe you'll find the terms generous," Cal finished. "Thanks for your time and your service to the magazine." He gave a brief—and Kit thought insincere—smile.

And with that he turned and left the room.

Chapter Three

This was not happening. It couldn't be happening. Surely God, Thor, Zeus and the rest of the Divine Justice League weren't so ticked about Kit's minor sins of the past—an overdue library book here, a little white lie about a man's prowess in bed there—that they'd let this happen.

Now of all times!

Well, she just couldn't let this happen. She didn't know how she was going to stop it, but she *had* to.

She remembered her own words to Johnny—was it just this afternoon? *You can't walk away every time a bully tries to take something from you.*

She couldn't walk away. She couldn't just *let* this guy pull her job out from under her. But how on earth could she stay? She'd been fired, for Pete's sake!

She watched, numb, as her friends and colleagues collected thick manila envelopes from a makeshift desk manned by a glossy-haired buxom brunette Kit had never seen before.

"Are you really going to take this without a fight?" Kit asked Lila Harper, author of a sewing column that had, perhaps, contained a few too many crocheted sweater-vests.

"The man said he doesn't need us anymore. No sense in fighting. Plus, I don't need the work, dear," Lila Harper said, patting Kit's shoulder with a thin paper-white hand.

No, of course she didn't. Neither did half the people here. They all either had other careers, well-paid spouses or retirement pensions. All the other staff members were in their twenties with no dependents or urgent considerations. For one ugly moment Kit felt as if she was the only one who really cared about keeping this job, the only one who needed it.

She continued to watch in disbelief as several of her other coworkers took their envelopes one by one and left as if they'd won some kind of prize. A slip-knot tightened in her stomach. It was over. She'd lost a battle without even realizing she was fighting.

Her house.

The little yard.

The school one block away.

The community pool with two diving boards.

All of it gone. Unless she could pull off some kind of miracle with this unapproachable man who seemed to have ice water running through his veins.

"Can you believe this?" Kathleen Browning asked, interrupting Kit's thoughts.

Kit looked at her and was gratified to see that the copy editor looked unhappy about the turn of events.

"No, I can't. I'm going to fight it," Kit said.

"How?"

The answer seemed so obvious. "I'm going to talk to this Panagos guy. I'm going to tell him I want to keep my job. Come with me. There's power in numbers."

Kathleen looked doubtful. "I don't know. Men like that make me nervous."

"Men like what?"

"He's so—" she sucked in her breath "—great-looking. If I try and talk to him, I'll probably just get nervous and pass out at his feet or something."

"Kathleen," Kit returned impatiently. "That's ridiculous. Look, I'll do most of the talking, you just come and agree with me."

Kathleen shook her head. "I don't think so. Actually I saw an ad for a fiction editor just last week and I think I'd like to try moving in that direction."

Wimp, Kit thought irritatedly.

"We'll get together soon," Fiona Whitcomb, the etiquette columnist, was saying to Lila as they shuffled behind Kit. "First Derek and I will probably go to Palm Springs for a few weeks of glorious sunshine."

Kit watched each of her old friends file out the door, shaking Cal's hand and smiling as they left. Who were these people? It was as if she hadn't known them at all. She half wondered if there were pods in the basement of the building, like in *Invasion of the Body Snatchers.*

Lucy took her envelope, opened it and gave a delighted exclamation, as if her Pepsi bottle cap had just declared her a winner.

Jo gave Kit a look, then stood up.

"Are you really going to do this?" Kit asked her.

"I don't have any choice," Jo said. "Look at that guy." She nodded toward Cal. "He means business. You can see there's no compromise there. He walked into this building intending to fire every one of us today and that's just what he did."

Kit felt as if she might cry. But she wouldn't. No way. "I'm going to change his mind about that."

Jo put her arm around her friend. "I bet you will,

too. I know this is really important to you, but don't forget there *are* other opportunities out there if you can't make this one work. You'll find a job and get that house."

There was no sense in pointing out that she needed *this* job *now* in order to get *this* loan at *this* interest rate. "What about you? Did you win the lottery or something? How come you don't need to worry about work?"

"I do, Kit, but I've been thinking about leaving this job lately anyway. I don't want to be Mr. Fix-It forever. There are better things out there for me. And if I get to leave here with a good recommendation and a severance package, I'm better off than I thought I'd be two weeks ago when I started seriously thinking of quitting."

Kit hadn't even realized her friend had been so close to quitting.

"Listen," Jo said, "if you want to stay and battle this out, I'll take Johnny home. We'll go to dinner and swing by your place later, okay?"

"Thanks," Kit said. For a moment she'd forgotten Johnny was still waiting in her office.

That was the kind of thoughtfulness that was going to make Kit really and truly miss seeing Jo at work every day. She'd been so lucky to work with her best friend for so long.

Now Kit was on her own. And she was going to go forward and change Cal Panagos's mind no matter what.

One by one the *Home Life* staff went until there were only two heartbeats left in the room: hers and Cal's. And she was pretty sure hers was faster.

Cal turned from the doorway and looked at Kit with what she saw now, on closer inspection, were piercing pale blue eyes. They were Newmanesque. This guy could be a movie star.

In fact, if he'd chosen that route, Kit would have been a lot better off.

"There's just one envelope left," he said to her in a voice that had probably melted lots of foolish women's hearts.

"Let me guess."

He gave a quick smile, the unexpectedness of which took her aback, and held the envelope out to her. "Thanks for your work, Ms. Macy."

She took a bracing breath and said, "I can't take that."

He cocked his head slightly. "I'm sorry?"

"I can't accept your severance package." She swallowed hard. She was suddenly self-conscious about her small, mousy self standing in front of him. She'd been in such a rush today that she hadn't done anything with her wild tangle of auburn hair. And she hadn't done the laundry in a few days and was wearing her Emergency Work Clothes, meaning gray pants that would have been a lot more flattering if she'd ever been able to stay on the South Beach Diet for more than two or three days.

Still, she had to work with what she had and she had to pretend she had confidence, even if at this particular moment she didn't.

"I need this job," she finished simply.

It was clear he hadn't been expecting an objection from anyone. He cleared his throat and said, "Well, I'm honestly sorry about this, but—"

She took a gamble. "Moreover, you need me."

He gave her look of dry query.

She nodded at his unasked question. "You do. I'm the only person who knows how to run this magazine. Okay," she conceded quickly, "things have been a little rocky here financially, but I know where we are with assignments right now and who needs to be contacted and so on. You wouldn't want to be sued for breach of contract." Shoot. She shouldn't have said that. She should have stopped while she was ahead.

From the look he gave her it was clear that Cal Panagos was not a man who liked being threatened, even in a veiled, passive-aggressive way.

He took a moment to straighten the lapel of his

Italian-tailored dark gray suit. It fit him perfectly, both physically and metaphorically. It was perfect and cold.

"Everyone needs to be contacted and all assignments need to be canceled," he said coolly. "My secretary can do that."

"Can your secretary find her way around the filing maze Lucy created? Some of our legal papers are filed under L for legal, but others are under S for *serious* legal."

Cal frowned as if he was trying to figure out whether Kit was on the level.

"Can your secretary figure out kill fees, which are different for each assignment and which are based on past history with each writer? The files are in a spreadsheet on my computer, but there are a lot of them to figure out. More to the point, do you want to pay her—or him—for the hours she'll have to spend trying to find her way through that maze? Or do you want to keep on the one person who can expedite it?"

He frowned again, drawing a dark shadow across the expression in his light blue eyes. "It may be hard for you to imagine, Ms. Macy, but, yes, I think I can do all of that—and more—without you." He tilted his head slightly. "After all, we've only just met. I've managed a much bigger publication than this without any guidance at all."

She'd taken the wrong tack. She needed to back off quick and try something different.

Maybe plain old honesty would do the trick.

It wasn't as if she had a lot of other options.

"Look," she said, "I'm not saying you and your staff aren't capable of these things. I'm just saying I'm *already* up to speed, so it makes a lot more sense, economically and timewise, to keep me on." She looked into his eyes, feeling as though she was swimming against the current in the turbulent ocean of his eyes. "It would benefit both of us."

His expression softened almost imperceptibly. Perhaps a slight turning of the tide. "Things are changing around here. A lot."

"I can change."

He raised an eyebrow slightly. This was a man who knew how he looked at all times and used it to communicate everything he wanted to say. "Are you willing to commit to doing it my way, even before you know what that means?"

She didn't have any choice. "Yes. Tell me what you want me to do and I'll do it. I'm a professional."

He nodded thoughtfully.

"Please." She bit the bullet so hard she wouldn't have been surprised if her teeth shattered. "I really need my job."

He was still holding the manila envelope with

her name on it. He looked at it, then back at her. A long moment passed before he dropped the envelope on the desk.

"This goes against my better judgment," he said.

Hope lurched in her chest. "Some of the best things in life begin with that very statement."

He raked his gaze across her. "You're a persuasive woman, Ms. Macy."

She smiled. "That will work to your advantage."

The smallest hint of a smile played at the curve of his mouth. "That particular feminine quality has occasionally worked against me in the past."

"Presumably you're referring to pleasure, not business."

He hesitated, looking at her. "Sometimes it's hard to separate the two."

A frisson of electricity zapped through her chest, and gooseflesh raised on her arms and against the cotton of her shirt. There was nothing to say he was talking about sex—he could have meant that he enjoyed his work so much that it was *always* a pleasure—but something about the way he looked at her gave Kit chills she didn't want to attribute to his sex appeal.

So she assigned it instead to a cool blast from the air conditioner.

Even though it was so muggy in the office that she couldn't be sure the air conditioner was even on.

"Well, I intend to make sure that working with me *is* a pleasure." Kit fumbled, hearing—probably at the same time he did—the clumsiness of her sentiment. "I mean, I think we'll work well together."

"There you go with that persuasion again," he said, with a smile that lit his pale blue eyes.

The air conditioner *had* to be on and she must be standing directly in front of a previously undetected vent, because she was positively getting *chills*. "Does that mean you're willing to give me a try?" she asked.

He gave a short laugh. "It's certainly tempting."

"I'm talking about the job."

He nodded for a long moment, then smiled and said, "Okay, you've got two months to prove yourself. If I can live without you by then, you're outta here. Period."

"Fine." She turned on her heel to leave when she remembered the call from the bank.

Oh, this wasn't going to be easy.

She turned back to Cal. "There's just one more thing," she said.

He looked at her wearily and let out a breath. "Don't tell me you want a raise."

She shook her head. "Just a letter to the bank assuring them that I'm gainfully employed." She gave a small shrug. "And if you could leave out the part about it being for two months, that would be great."

* * *

Cal watched the feisty redhead leave the room and shook his head. The girl was trouble, every nerve in his body told him so. The way she raised that chin and leveled those Kelly-green eyes at him—she was like a kitten, irrationally brave in the face of the wolf who could eat her alive.

Then she'd flounced out of the place, after having the nerve to ask him to put in writing that he employed her, with her long tangle of hair swinging behind her like spun copper. He had to admire her nerve, as crazy at it was. Hell, he was tempted to tell the bank he was paying her four times what she earned just because she'd taken the chance on asking him.

She was a nervy little thing.

And he could eat her alive all right.

For the time being, though, he'd resist that. She could flit around the office and pull files and make calls. He could use that. Maybe she'd even live up to her own advertising, though in Cal's experience it was rare that a woman that pretty had the smarts to back it up.

His only real concern about keeping her was that she might prove to be too much of a distraction to him. He had a lot to do and almost no time to do it. In the past he'd had the leisure to flirt and enjoy the chase. He'd also had the security of a large number of personnel, so when the flirting was done and the chase was over, he could disappear back into the excuse of business and that would be that.

But at the moment Kit Macy was his only employee, and given the modest—no, *meager*—budget Breck Monahan had allowed, he wasn't going to be able to hire more than fifteen or twenty more.

Hardly the sort of numbers that would allow him to back off gracefully at the end of a fling.

So there would be no fling.

He could live with that.

He got up and went to the back room where Ebbit Markham had pointed out a hundred-odd years' worth of back issues of the magazine. It was musty and dark, and it occurred to Cal that he might be better off just lighting the whole lot on fire or locking the door and throwing away the key.

The unpleasantness of the room—of the whole damned chaotic and failing office, actually—was the perfect metaphor for the present state of his career.

How the hell had he let this happen? All his life Cal had succeeded wherever he'd tried. A psychologist could have a field day with his motivation—Cal's father had died when Cal was just seven, leaving him alone to be the man of the house for his mother and sister—but whatever the reason, he'd always felt really *good* about his success. He'd *enjoyed* winning, whether it was class valedictorian or the Presidential Young Entrepreneur Award or a full scholarship to Stanford.

Winning was who he was. Who he'd always been.

And all the stuff that went with it now—the nice co-op, a good car, thirty-year-old scotch in the cupboard—was proof of his achievements. The stuff itself wasn't his goal, it was just the certificate on the wall.

He'd grown to appreciate it for that.

Now not only were his finances on the line—he could always make money again—but it was also his reputation. The reputation he'd spent a lifetime building, polishing.

If that went down in flames with *Home Life* he might never recover it.

So what was he doing in this crummy old building downtown trying to resurrect a business that had been terminally ill for half a century? Sure, he'd made a mistake—and it was just that, a *mistake*—but did he really deserve this kind of punishment?

If he'd had any time at all, he might have really felt ticked off about it. But as it was, he had to just step up to the plate and knock one out of the park.

So he'd do what he could, beginning with the one employee he had so far.

He'd gone to the archives with Kit Macy in mind. Now that she was gone and he wasn't diverted by her obvious physical…assets, he could look at her work and try and determine if in fact there was any promise there.

Hell, maybe she *could* help him rescue this dog of a magazine. She probably couldn't hurt.

Unless he let her.

His libido had gotten him into trouble before, God knew, and even today he'd tried to stop himself from letting Kit stick around and make his life harder. But in the end he just hadn't been able to do it. There was something about her—he really couldn't even say exactly what it was. It didn't even matter now because he'd already said he'd give her a chance.

So maybe, just maybe, he'd find something in her work that would make him feel as if for once his head and his libido were both right about the same woman.

Chapter Four

"As we sit with our toes in the hot sand, it occurs to me that our lives are reflected perfectly in nature. The ebb and flow of the ocean mirrors our lives in the most straightforward way possible. There is good and there is bad, there is high and there is low. The only thing you can truly count on is you will face both. Over and over again." Cal stopped reading and set last month's issue of the magazine down on his desk before looking Kit in the eye. "This is what you've been doing these past five years?"

"No. Two and a half. When Edith died, I took over the job until we could find someone new, but then—" she shrugged "—I just kept doing it. We decided to just keep her byline on it."

"Did you have any writing experience prior to that?"

"I majored in English in college," she offered, knowing instantly that he thought that was feeble. "And of course I've done a lot of editing on the magazine."

"So this woman died and you inserted yourself—someone with no writing experience—in her place? No interviews? No trying to get the best person for the job?"

"Well, having been her most recent editor, I knew her style," Kit said, caught off guard by his judgment that she'd done something potentially unethical. "Ebbit felt I was the best person to replace her and I was glad to do it. Writing is one of the things I've enjoyed most about working here. It really helps me understand both sides of the job."

"But *that* is exactly what's wrong here. *Home Life* is an outdated publication, written at least in part by dead people because it's more convenient than getting new talent."

Kit worked to keep her temper in check. "But we were doing what our readers wanted."

"What makes you think so?"

"We've gotten letters. They've been reading that

column for *years.*" She brought out what she thought was a good point. "Since before you were born."

"Exactly." He jabbed a finger in the air toward her. "*Exactly.* Your demographics stink. Your audience is literally dying."

Kit protested despite the knowledge that Cal had *definitely* scored with that remark. "That's not fair—"

"Anyone who's been reading *Home Life* since before I was born is way too old to attract lucrative advertising. That's why sales are down. *Home Life* just isn't relevant anymore. If it ever was."

"We have two million subscribers who feel otherwise," Kit said heatedly.

"And there are at *least* five or six million potential subscribers who agree with me." He shook his head. "You've been writing and publishing this June Cleaver, *Christmas in Connecticut* stuff without regard to the fact that we've started a new millennium." He gestured at the article. "No one lives like that anymore. Hell, I don't think they ever did."

How could he have missed her point so completely? "That was sort of the idea. To create an escape, a fantasy for my readers. A haven from this crazy world."

"But *that* isn't the fantasy anymore. It hasn't been for thirty or forty years. The whole 'happy homemaker' idea is outdated, irrelevant." He stopped and leveled a cool blue gaze on her. "And worst of all, it's boring. I'm sorry."

He didn't sound sorry at all.

She could have punched him for his tone, even while part of her knew he was right. Her writing had appealed to her own fantasies but she knew most people weren't as old-fashioned as she. She'd always been a bit of a throwback. "So what is it you think our readers want?"

"Oprah. Tina Brown. Nigella Lawson." He fired them off rapidly. "Women today have it all and wield their power from the bedroom to the boardroom. They want their success validated, their hard work rewarded. And in their downtime, they want some fast-food modern spirituality and good old raunchy gossip."

"Gossip?"

"Sure. The bare naked truth about all those supposed style icons out there." He stopped and jotted something down on the paper in front of him. "Women today aren't as naive as their 1950s counterparts. That homey ideal might be nice, but it just doesn't have a genuine place in their lives."

It was as if he was shooting teeny tiny arrows at her with every word. She liked her homey ideal. She'd considered it timeless, not outdated. Yet she knew that in reality she was in the minority. The public didn't share her mind-set, for the most part. She'd known that for a while now, even while she'd told herself she was providing something valuable.

Listening to Cal, she realized it was just…quaint.

And quaint wouldn't cut it.

Now if she wanted to keep her job—and there was no *if* about it, she *had* to keep her job—she was going to have to do everything she could around there to make herself valuable. She'd do a column, be the managing editor, be the janitor if she had to.

And if she was going to do a column for this new incarnation of the magazine, she was going to have to change her whole personality to fit Cal Panagos's corporate image of the modern woman. She was going to have to turn from innocent Sandy in the beginning of *Grease* to sexy, savvy Sandy at the end without even enough time for the wardrobe change.

"I can give you what you want," Kit said evenly.

"Not in the office," he said pointedly.

A lesser person would have shot right back with a comment about sexual harassment.

And a better person might have resisted the little thrill of pleasure at what his meaning *might* have been.

And a *different* person would have known how to tell the difference between an innocent comment and a not-so-innocent comment and would have been absolutely clear on how she should feel about both.

"Yes, I can," she said, meeting his gaze evenly. Let *him* try and figure out what *she* meant for once. "In the office or at home, I can do my job." Though in truth, she wasn't a hundred percent sure of that. Sometime over the past few days the world had changed without letting her know. She wasn't sure what her place in it was anymore or what she could do with what she had.

Cal leaned back in his chair. "If you can be half as determined to keep up with the times as you are to prove I'm wrong, you might succeed here."

"Really?"

"Sure. If you can stop being Donna Reed, I think you might have something to say to the women in our demographic."

She had to smile. He wasn't *quite* as icy as she'd thought at first. Behind the slick veneer there was a thinking man who wanted to succeed.

Of course, she knew that from the moment she first saw him. And she confirmed it when she went home that night and looked him up on the Internet. Henry Carl Panagos had been the youngest editor in chief ever on *Sports Life* magazine and he had lifted sagging sales by changing the format to shorter, punchier pieces and adding quick-reference charts of the professional sports seasons past and present. He'd also taken the innovative step of having some of the sports greats themselves do profiles of up-and-comers, including New York Giants great linebacker Lawrence Taylor on Ray Lewis.

In fact, in four years on the job Cal hadn't appeared to make a false step.

So what was he doing at *Home Life* of all places?

Kit could only surmise that Breck Monahan had sent the boy wonder over to perform a miracle.

Well, she was going to be an integral part of that miracle. "Who exactly do you see as the women of our demographic?" she asked him.

He leaned forward, as if ready to launch into a favorite subject. "Women like you. Your age. Your situation."

"Meaning…?"

"Working mom. Someone said you have a kid."

"I do. I have a son."

"And—" he hesitated for just a fraction of a second "—no husband, right?"

She hesitated, as well.

She wasn't sure what either of their hesitations meant.

"Not anymore."

He gave a one-shoulder shrug. "There are ten million single mothers in the U.S."

"At least."

"To say nothing of fourteen million working mothers with partners and five million stay-at-home moms." He'd done his research, that much was obvious. And it was impressive. "That's thirty million readers to whom our magazine could and should be *completely* relevant."

He was right. Thirty million potential readers under the age of sixty trumped twenty-one million potential geriatric readers. "You're right."

"So find out what interests them and do it," he said. "Entertainment, sex—I don't care what, just make it relevant. Find the writers who will make it relevant."

"Okay," she said slowly, gathering her nerve. "With that in mind, I want to keep writing my column."

The word *no* showed up immediately on his face, and she hastened to add, "What I mean is, a *new* column. New slant. But I want to keep writing."

He lifted the copy of her column that he'd just set down. "I don't think you've got the tone I'm looking for."

"No, *Edith* didn't have the tone you were looking for. You have no idea what I can do."

He took a short breath and looked her over. "Tell me about it."

"I know what you want now," Kit told him confidently. She'd been in the business world long enough to know how to play businesswoman. "And I can deliver."

"Can you?"

"Absolutely."

"Why do you want to?"

That threw her off. "I beg your pardon?"

"Why do you want to do this?" he repeated.

"Do what exactly? Write the column?"

He nodded. "If you're already working as the managing editor, why do you want to add more work to your load?"

"Well…" She was unsure whether or not she should tip her hand but decided she had nothing to lose. "That part of my job accounts for a third of my income."

"You realize that's not a particularly compelling reason for me to keep you on in that area."

"Yes." She wasn't good at this business of constantly selling herself. "But in turn I'm sure *you* realize that you have a particularly motivated worker here. One you should recognize as a serious bargain."

He looked amused. "How do you figure that?"

"It's to my advantage to make myself as difficult to replace as possible. If I can do two jobs for one price, then why would you want to sack me and hire two people to replace me?" Not to mention that those columns, under her own name, would make a nice portfolio if/when she really did have to leave this place.

He gave a laugh. "Good point. Except for the fact that you've been doing those two jobs in such a way that hasn't resulted in sales for the magazine. Why would I hire one person at one price and continue to tank if by hiring two more people and unloading the first I can increase revenues tenfold?"

Kit cleared her throat. He was right and she had to make him feel wrong somehow. "Mr. Panagos, I've done what I was instructed to do. My work was absolutely in line with the tone of the magazine. Had I done something new and innovative—along the lines you might prefer—it could have alienated our readers."

He tapped his finger against his chin. "In other words, you're a good worker but not an independent thinker."

"That's not what I said."

He shrugged. "It's what I heard."

She stifled her exasperation. "I'm an independent thinker but not a fool. I did what the previous editor in chief wanted me to do. You want something entirely different. I get that."

"Then the question is, will you do it?"

"Absolutely."

He looked at her, turned the corners of his mouth down and gave a nod. "Okay. You've got one chance. Let's see, today is Monday, so—" he glanced at his desk calendar "—have it on my desk by next Monday morning."

Chapter Five

That night Kit tried to see her column with the cold, judgmental eye she attributed to Cal. She read it to Joanna as they sipped cheap white wine in Kit's living room.

"November brings chill winds and clear cold nights, making it a perfect time to take your family indoors and cuddle up by the fire. Warm soup, spicy chili and sweet pumpkin pies (see page 35) are just some of the treats you can serve your hungry crew."

"I could use some chili right now," Jo interjected.

Kit shot her a look and read on. "Steve is in the backyard now, chopping wood for the winter. Johnny is collecting golden leaves for a door wreath (see page 44). And I have a big pot of vegetable soup on the stove. I look forward to a cozy night by the fire; even as we're melancholy about letting go of summer, winter holds out her arms to us. This is a time to welcome change and look forward to the possibilities it brings." She stopped and looked at Joanna. "He's right."

"Who's right?"

"Cal Panagos. This stinks. No one lives like this. That's why we all hate Martha Stewart."

"I don't hate Martha Stewart!"

"Yes, you do. Every woman does on some level." She tossed the column aside. "We want to be superwomen. All-powerful. I am *woman*." She struck a mock pose, flexing her biceps.

"Roar, sister." Jo laughed. "Hey, that reminds me, I'm going to a sex-toy party next Tuesday. Want to come with me? Please? I can't do it alone."

Kit crooked an eyebrow at her pal. "A sex-toy party."

Jo shrugged. "Hey, my college roommate has started doing these things to make extra money. Besides, it's something I've never done before. Could be interesting."

"I'm *sure* it will be interesting." Kit laughed. "But

I'm not sure that's my kind of thing. When I get lonely, I tend to turn on the TV."

Jo chuckled. "Been watching a lot of Nick at Nite lately?"

Kit sighed. "Tons. I can recite almost every line of every episode of *The Brady Bunch*."

"You know, now that you've gotten this hunky new boss, maybe you should think about a little more fun at the office, if you know what I mean."

She did know. Over the past several hours she'd caught herself thinking about it way more than she wanted to. It wasn't hard to slip into fantasies about Cal Panagos.

"I don't see him that way," she said, imagining Cal coming out of the shower, a white towel wrapped around his narrow hips, his golden skin gleaming under droplets of water.

"Really? He's pretty hot."

"Hmm." Kit tried to sound as if she hadn't actually thought of him that way. "All I know is that he's ice-cold when it comes to business." And she imagined running an ice cube over that warm, wet skin.

"Sometimes that can be attractive."

"What can?"

"That cool exterior. There's usually a steaming-hot sex god underneath it, you know. That kind of man might be *exactly* what you need right now."

Right now, after a couple of glasses of wine, it felt as if Cal Panagos *was* exactly what she needed. Mentally she dropped the ice cube and Cal dropped the towel and they came together in a kiss so hot it could melt lips.

Then they lowered *slowly* through the steam to the cool tile floor, where Cal took her with a passion that gentle, timid Rick had never even approached.

"Kit? Hello?"

Mortified that she'd gotten lost in those thoughts, Kit jerked her attention to Jo. "What?"

"Wow, you were like a million miles away. What were you thinking about?"

Oh, no. Had she moaned? Pursed her lips? It had been so long since she'd been with a man that she'd almost thought she didn't have a libido anymore. Was it Cal that brought it out in her or the wine? And was Jo on to her? "I was just thinking about how hard it's going to be to actually work with Cal Panagos day to day."

Jo seemed to accept that at face value. "Then you really should come to the party with me. You never know if you're going to need to think about a new career."

Relieved to change the subject, Kit asked, "Are you saying you're considering this instead of going back to art school?"

Jo laughed heartily. "No, not yet. Besides, Parker says if I ever need a job, I can join him in his Web design business. Apparently there's a lot of potential for income there, as well as creativity. Plus, we could work together."

"Oh, that's so sweet!" Kit was all for anything that got Jo to spend more time with Parker. He was the first boyfriend Jo had had in a long time who wasn't a soul-sucking man-child. "Maybe you should consider it."

"I would if he had any work at all."

"Oh."

"Yeah, *oh*. Potential doesn't mean much when you've got nothing. Besides, I'm a semester away from having a degree in graphic arts. I don't know why I ever quit in the first place, but I'm going to finish this time."

Kit shrugged. "You couldn't resist the lure of *Home Life*. The glamour, the excitement, the notoriety, the—"

"Smell of Ben-Gay permeating the office," Jo finished for her.

Kit made a face. It was true, there was no denying it.

"Mommy?" Johnny's sleepy voice interrupted, eradicating any lingering thoughts Kit might have had of hitting the floor naked with Cal.

Kit turned to see him stumbling sleepily into the room. "What is it, honey?"

"I had a bad dream." He held one arm up in front of his eyes to shield them from the light. In the other hand he held the battered Buzz Lightyear doll. One of Buzz's hands had broken off and the swivel in his helmet was a little loose, but the voice buttons still worked like new, as did the grating laser sound he was emitting right now.

"Okay." Kit put her arms out. "Stop with the laser and come sit with me for a few minutes while I talk to Joanna. You can go right back to sleep in my lap, okay?"

Johnny walked straight to her, bonked her in the knees with Buzz and held his arms up for her to lift him.

She did, carefully removing his small finger from the laser button, and carried him over to the big, overstuffed rocker. She sat down, and her son curled into her arms like the baby he'd been not so long ago.

"So you were saying?" Joanna prompted in a quiet voice. "I mean about Panagos. You were saying you agree with him."

"Oh, yes. That. I agree that what I was doing wasn't working." Before Jo felt as if she needed to reassure Kit on that point, Kit added, "It's obvious. The circulation numbers prove that."

"Okay. So what approach will you take?"

"Every approach. I'm going to read, watch and look at everything I can think of that might point me in the direction of the next trends in thought."

"I am Buzz Lightyear, space ranger."

Kit sighed and gently but firmly moved Johnny's hand away from the voice buttons. "I'm open to anything people are interested in right now."

"Did I mention this party I'm going to?" Jo smiled.

"I believe you did."

Johnny stirred in Kit's arms and drew the heavy doll closer, clocking himself in the chin in the process.

"I come in peace."

"Johnny," Kit said softly, "keep Buzz still so he stops making noise."

"I didn't do anything," Johnny argued, turning in her lap and knocking the doll against the chair.

"Stand by while I set my lasers to stun."

Exasperated, Kit put a hand on the toy to keep it still.

Joanna gestured toward Kit with her wineglass. "Have you seen that book on meditations for women who are too busy? *Stop and Sit with the Roses?*"

"It's on my bedside table."

"Have you read it?"

"I haven't had time!"

Jo laughed.

"But I will. Honest." Kit sipped her wine. "I have to if I want to keep working. I have to find out what American women are thinking and dealing with and I need to address it with honesty. And humor. And a little extra zing that other writers aren't delivering right now."

"If anyone can do it, you can."

"To infinity...and beyond!"

Kit removed the toy from Johnny's hand completely and set it on the floor, adding, "Remind me of that every once in a while, would you?"

"Absolutely. To Kit Macy and having your finger on the pulse of the American woman." Jo raised her glass. "But when you put your finger on her pulse, be careful not to wake her up. From what I can tell, she really needs the sleep."

Chapter Six

Kit's Diary
Home Life *magazine*
November 2005 issue

In this day and age, when we're more frantic than ever, it's vitally important to take time out for ourselves. Psychologist Dr. Melanie Sherwood suggests an hour of private "morning meditation" every day, before the rest of the family rises. It may be hard to get up at five in the morning at first, but—

"What crap." Kit hit the shift key and scrolled over everything she'd written, then, with some vehemence, hit delete. She wasn't attaching her name to such drivel.

Dr. Melanie, as she was known to her many radio listeners, was an idiot. There was no way she had kids, that much was obvious. And probably no husband, because if there was a man out there who was worth having sex with at night after you'd been up since five in the morning, working and being Mommy, Kit hadn't met him. After a day like that, she'd even kick Brad Pitt out of bed if it meant getting an extra half hour of sleep.

Kit leaned back and looked at the white computer screen. The cursor blinked like the turn signal on an old Chevy going twenty miles an hour in the left lane of the information superhighway.

She pushed back from the desk and went to put on another pot of coffee. She'd already had three cups since Joanna had left, but with no result. Maybe she was caffeine-immune. It was only ten-thirty at night, but after a day as stressful as the one she'd had, nothing but sleep could wake her up.

On the other hand, maybe the mental fatigue of creating a whole new set of lies to feed women— "You can do it all and be happy!"—was just too much weight to bear. Her subconscious had to resort to narcolepsy in order to stop her.

Why were people buying this? Why did women think they needed to do it all and make everyone else happy in the process? Of the four current self-help bestsellers Kit had tried to read, she'd thrown three across the room in anger, and Dr. Melanie was about to join them. Telling people that they could do it all—or should even try—was a lie. A dangerous lie.

"Edith's Diary" had been full of lies, too, of course, but at least it had been harmless. She'd never tried to tell women they should get up at five in the morning to grab an hour for themselves before making a full breakfast and bag lunches for the family, commuting in traffic, working eight or more hours in an office, commuting in more traffic, making dinner for four from scratch, cleaning up, reading bedtime stories and slipping into a black negligee to please a husband. How could anyone function with a schedule like that? It was a wonder that the news wasn't full of stories of women opening fire in the workplace.

But no. They were probably too tired for homicide. Most of the women Kit knew just kept trying and quietly hoped that someday, maybe when the kids were grown, things would get better. Someday they could take off the leaden suits of exhaustion they wore and sleep for several days straight, making up for all the sleep lost during the Mother Years. Everyone, she suspected, secretly worried that they were the only one not succeeding at doing it all.

She needed to write about *this*.

When the phone rang in the midst of these thoughts, Kit knew it could only be one person. A quick glance at the caller ID confirmed it. "Hello, mother."

"No time to chat, dear, I just had to find out about him firsthand."

"Who?"

"Breck Monahan! I saw on TV that he bought your magazine. Have you met him yet?"

"No, and I don't think I'm going to. He owns the magazine, but he's not really what you'd call hands-on. He hired someone else to run the magazine."

"Yes, your father mentioned that. A fellow who used to work for that sports magazine your father orders every year so he can get a phone shaped like a football."

"Sports Life," Kit supplied and realized, for the first time since meeting Cal, that *Sports Life* was the magazine she'd given her dad for Christmas a couple of times when she was a kid. That would have been before Cal's time, of course, but still the symmetry of it struck her as interesting.

"*I* thought they should have put *you* in charge," Kit's mother went on. "You've been there so long you could probably do it in your sleep."

Kit immediately imagined Cal's response: they *had* been doing it in their sleep. That was a big part of the problem.

Oh-oh. She already had Cal's voice in her head. This was not good.

"As a matter of fact, I think I'll write a letter telling Breck Monahan exactly that. He's a fool to ignore your talents when you're right there under his nose."

"Oh, no, please don't do that, Mom. Please. Seriously." She pictured the letter, on her mother's trademark pale blue stationery, landing on Cal's desk along with the mere four or five other pieces of mail they typically got in a day. "I really like the guy in charge and, believe me, I would *not* want that job."

"Okay." Her mother sounded doubtful. "If you're sure."

"I'm sure. Honestly—" Kit's response was interrupted by Steve lurching into her office, his stomach croaking like rusty riggings on a ship.

He was about to puke.

"Sorry, Mom. I have to go."

"Is something wrong?"

"No, it's fine. I'll call you later." She threw the phone down. "Get out! Come on, out, out, *out!*" She pushed the heaving dog from behind, straight to the front door. She was fumbling to open the dead bolt, like a game show contestant trying to unlock a prize box with one of ten keys in only five seconds, when the dog spilled his cookies—or rather Johnny's cookies, if the color was any indication—all over the hall floor.

For a minute she just stood there staring at it.

She was *not* in the mood for this. She was never in the mood for this, but it had been a long, long day. Joanna had gone, Johnny had finally returned to his bedroom, Kit had sobered up and stopped fantasizing about Cal and all she wanted to do now was write. But this—*this* couldn't be ignored. It wouldn't just go away.

She had never missed having a husband more.

Steve looked at her with guilty eyes. As if he understood.

Her heart softened. "Poor Steve," she said, patting him gingerly on the head. "Come on, go outside." She opened the door and let him out. He had a routine. He'd go down the cement steps to the five square feet of common-area grass in front of the apartment building, sit down and survey the neighborhood, then come back to the front step in a few minutes. That would give her time to clean up the mess.

She went back to the kitchen, grabbed a roll of

paper towels and a plastic bag and cleaned the mess up as well as she could without really looking, shoving the paper towels into the bag and tying it quickly. She took the bag to the trash can outside, then came back to the kitchen to find the Lysol.

This, she thought, was what modern home life was *really* like. All those books—*Stop and Sit with the Roses, Dr. Melanie's Guide to Womanly Fulfillment, Secret Abandon: Tapping into a Woman's Inner Life*—all of them were full of absurd advice to get up early, stay up late, listen to monks chanting for inner peace and burn eighty-dollar serenity candles next to a bathtub full of rose petals. Soon Martha Stewart—or the Next Martha Stewart—would come out with a book on how to create time out of ingredients you already have around the home.

It was ridiculous.

There was going to be a backlash. Possibly sooner rather than later. Women everywhere were going to stand up and revolt against the afternoon talk show lies about what they should be doing.

And Kit was more than willing to lead the charge.

She opened the cabinet under the sink and threw the Lysol back, closing the door quickly so the contents of the closet didn't all come spilling out. She stepped away from the cabinet and heard the contents behind the door shift.

That would come back to haunt her the next time she opened up the cabinet.

She walked away thinking about the more immediate predicament. She couldn't, she realized all at once with absolute conviction, join the bandwagon in telling women to kill themselves in the name of fulfillment.

Plus, she believed with every fiber of her weary being that if she did what Cal wanted, she would fall on her sword and be out at the end of her two months. Her only chance was to do something *different,* something that no one else was doing.

She was going to tell the truth about life as a working mother.

After all, what mother *wasn't* a working mother? Everyone could relate on some level.

Diary of a Domestic Goddess
Ten Things I Never Thought I'd Have to Say
(or Motherhood Changes Everything)

1. "Stop licking the wall."
2. "If you don't eat your broccoli now, I'm calling Santa Claus. And no, you can't have a lollipop. At all."
3. "Take the trash can off your head."
4. "Stop putting your peas in your ears. I said, *stop putting your peas in your ears!*"

5. "Mrs. Leonard knows her bottom popped, you don't to need tell her."

6. "Just one bite of broccoli. One. Then you can have a lollipop."

7. "Stop wiping your runny nose on the dog."

8. "We don't need to be quiet because your foot's asleep."

9. "Changing your name to Superman does NOT give you the ability to fly. Don't EVER try that again."

10. "Oh, fine, go ahead and eat the lollipop."

It was all Marjorie Sears's fault.

That's why Cal had kept Kit Macy on at the magazine even while his instincts told him to start the whole thing over from the ground up. Kit reminded him of Marjorie, his high school girlfriend. Earnest. Determined even in the face of utter failure. Sexy as hell even when she was mad. Marjorie hadn't given him an inch more than kissing throughout the four years he'd known her, so naturally she loomed large in his memory now. Anyone who reminded him of her automatically had his attention.

Even if it was to his detriment.

It was a mistake to keep her, of course. He'd wrestled with it since the moment she'd left his office swinging her hips like a 1940s pinup come to life.

What he needed, rather than this hot curvaceous woman, was an ambitious young go-getter. A thinker. Someone who could come up with the angles no one else would think of. Someone hungry for success and ruthless about going for it.

That wasn't Kit. It never would be. Kit was a sexy old-fashioned mom; she wasn't the sharp, edgy workaholic he needed in her place.

His phone rang and he moved to look at the caller ID.

It was Monahan.

Eleven o'clock on a Monday night and Monahan was calling him at home. The jackass.

For a moment Cal considered not answering, but he knew Monahan would just keep calling. He pushed the talk button. "Cal Panagos."

"How are things at *Home Life?*" Breck Monahan barked across the line. "You get rid of all the old employees, send them packing?"

Translation: *Did you do my dirty work for me?*

"Most of them," Cal said. "Yeah."

"Most?"

If Cal wasn't willing to fire Kit Macy himself, he sure as hell wasn't going to let Monahan do it. "I fired them. All gone."

"How soon are you going to bring us into the black?"

Cal leaned his head against the window and looked at the car headlights and brake lights on Broadway three stories below. "Four months, Breck. Isn't that what we talked about?"

"This is a hell of an investment, Panagos. I don't have that kind of time."

"That's bull, Breck, and you know it. You could afford to let this carp float on the water for years." Just this morning Cal had seen a piece on Monahan's acquisition in the *Wall Street Journal.* It had been a huge media merger, even more so than Cal had thought at first. *Home Life* was just a tiny, superfluous part of it. Hell, it hadn't even been mentioned by name in the article. It just fell under the umbrella of "and other publications."

"Maybe I could." Breck gave a mirthless laugh. "But you can't. You've got three months."

"With the production schedule in place, that's *one* issue of the magazine. If I'm lucky. You know damn well that no one could turn it around *that* fast!"

And Breck did know it. It was all part of his plan. "If you don't do it by then, it's over. You can't say I didn't give you a chance. No one could at that point." The phone clicked and melted to a dial tone.

Cal pushed the off button and tossed the receiver onto the sofa and looked back out at the traffic. He loved this view. He'd worked hard for it. It was one more symbol of how he was rewarded for his hard work. One more symbol that he had a purpose in this world.

Now it looked as if it might just slip through his fingers.

And it was all his own fault.

His libido had landed him square on the deck of this sinking ship. He'd learned his lesson the hard way: one lecherous employer—Monahan—with one hot but secret mistress who ended up in Cal's bed plus five, six, seven beers at the company party minus good discretion equals one ticked off boss.

Big mistake, as it turned out.

And the hell of it was that it shouldn't have been *that* big a deal. Romantic dalliances weren't necessarily something to be rewarded, but if they didn't interfere with a guy's work performance they shouldn't be held against him.

Too bad Monahan didn't see it that way.

No, Monahan was just looking for an excuse to sack Cal now. Obviously he figured he had it all sewn up when he put Cal at the helm of the sinking *Home Life.* How could it possibly succeed at this point?

And how could Monahan keep an editor in chief of such a miserable failure?

Three months. He wasn't even sure God could save this magazine in that amount of time.

Actually he wasn't even sure God was on his side in the endeavor.

So he was on his own. Completely.

Except for Kit Macy, a small voice in his head reminded him. The one person who was willing to cling to the rotting sides of this sinking ship. Maybe she had enough savvy in her to at least give him a solid foundation to work from these first couple of days. He was a fast study—it wouldn't take long for him to pick up on the filing system and the kill fees and anything else that was going on in the failing publication.

Which would be a good thing, because his life depended on the success of *Home Life,* as pitiful as that was. If he failed, he could kiss his job, his home, his car, his reputation and his future goodbye.

And he could give a good long welcome hug to the unemployment line.

He knew what he had to do. He had to get a premier issue of the reformatted magazine out there almost immediately. It was going to take some fast and meticulous planning, but that might be his only shot.

He went to the kitchen and put on a pot of coffee. It was going to be a long night.

By morning he had to have a new mission statement. By afternoon he had to have a new staff.

Which brought his thoughts back to Kit Macy. The one holdover from the old *Home Life* staff. The single person who could either help or hinder his efforts. Probably both. But it was the hindrance that concerned him more. The distraction.

The hedonistic thoughts that were creeping across his best intentions.

It wasn't just the Marjorie Sears thing that had gotten to him, though she had the same gleaming chestnut hair and soft build that made her pretty damn fine to look at.

No, it was something else. Kit Macy had intelligence in her eyes, and that intrigued him. She also argued with him, which no one else did. He kind of admired that. She'd have been an interesting one to have around for a while.

It was a real shame he would have to fire her eventually.

Chapter Seven

The writers were already lining up. So far, Cal had hired two notable names to do pieces on travel and technology. These were names that would draw readers, which meant it was stiff competition for Kit. If she didn't do something good and different, there was no way in the world Cal would let her write.

And if she didn't write, she'd be just another office administrator. So if the new and hopefully improved *Home Life* failed—as everyone seemed to believe it would—Kit would have only administrative work to point to in order to get a new job. Her work as "Edith Chamberlain" wasn't going to bring in any great opportunities as a writer or columnist elsewhere.

She *had* to do something. Something sincere. Something Cal couldn't say was derivative of someone else's work.

An hour after she began Kit had deleted entire screens' worth of work at least ten times.

Then the phone rang. She welcomed the interruption so much that even if it was an opinion pollster, she was prepared to sit down and chat for twenty minutes.

To her surprise, though, it was Cal. "Can you come down to the office today?"

"It's Saturday." Didn't she have something going on tonight? Nothing very interesting, of course, but wasn't there *something?*

She glanced at the refrigerator and remembered. A couple that she and Rick used to go out with now and then had invited her to a cocktail party that night. The invitation was stuck to the fridge door with a magnet. She'd kept it just in case she felt desperate to get out, but the handwritten scrawl at the bottom of the card had put her off. *No children please! Thanks!*

Kit would never have presumed to bring Johnny to a cocktail party anyway, but the fact that they went out of their way to exclude him ticked her off.

"Desperation has no holidays," Cal said. "I thought you were on board with getting the magazine in shape."

She smiled privately. Given the single obnoxious invitation on her fridge, it wasn't as if she had anything more compelling to do. Johnny was with Rick, and Kit wasn't getting anywhere with her writing.

And the thought of spending the afternoon with Cal Panagos wasn't exactly torture. Even though she knew the very fact that she could warm to the idea was a warning to her.

Because obviously it wasn't personal. She wasn't interested in Cal himself. How could she be? He was arrogant, bossy, insensitive and self-centered. She could tell that already.

Yes, he was good-looking. Really good-looking. Great-looking, if one wanted to get technical.

And therein lay the rub—Kit's libido was finally starting to muster some life after several years of dormancy and it had dropped its attention directly on the first attractive man who had happened along.

In this case, Cal Panagos.

She was on to her own subconscious's tricks.

So she simply needed to remind herself that Cal Panagos was a placeholder for the man who was obviously coming into her life in the near future. Cal Panagos was a practice run, starting up the creaky engine of her sex drive.

It was simple psychology.

And in the meantime she couldn't lose sight of the fact that she could use every bit of overtime she could get.

"Sure, I'll come down. Is two o'clock okay?"

"Can you make it one?"

Honestly, sometimes it seemed as if he was so determined to have things happen on his terms that it didn't even matter to him if his needs were practical.

"No, but I can make it at two."

Cal knew when he had the lower hand, apparently. "That's fine. I'll see you then. Oh, and Kit?"

"Yes?"

"Could you pick up something to eat on the way in? Maybe a pastrami on rye, no mayo?"

She'd have liked to refuse, but a pastrami on rye with no mayonnaise sounded *perfect* to her, too, and it would be just plain obnoxious for her to pick one up for herself but refuse to get him one, too.

"Tomato?" she asked, hoping she didn't sound too accommodating. After all, she didn't want him asking her to make coffee for him next.

"Tomato and onion," he said. "That sounds good."

Yes, it did. It was as if he was in her head. "You got it," she told him. "I'll see you at two or so."

She hung up the phone feeling strangely hungry.

But somehow she wasn't sure a sandwich was going to fully satiate her at this point.

Kit arrived in the office at two o'clock on the dot. It was her lot in life to be flawlessly punctual. Even when she wasn't trying, nine times out of ten she'd arrive just as the digital clock clicked to the minute.

Cal was waiting for her when she got there. "Got the sandwich?" he asked like a kidnapper asking for ransom.

"Here." She handed him the white paper bag from Cole's Deli. "You owe me seven-fifty-three."

"Fifty-*three?*"

"Tax."

He took a ten out of his wallet and handed it to her, then scoffed at her when she started to try and make change. "Did you already eat?"

She nodded, putting her wallet away in her purse. "On the way. I was starving."

"Good." He reached for a clipboard with several sheets of paper bound in. "Then you can get up to speed while you're waiting for me."

She looked at the clipboard as he passed it to her. It was a series of questions: *What is the most important quality in a man? How much does size matter to you? Would you rather have sex or a day off?*

Have you ever considered hiring an escort?

Kit stopped reading and looked at him, mouth agape. "I am *not* filling this out."

He took a big, untidy bite of his sandwich. "Yes, you are," he said with his mouth full. "So am I. I have one, too." He nodded toward a second clipboard on the desk.

He was going to fill out a survey about men? Was he…? No… Could Kit really have misread him *that* completely? Her heart sank right into her sandwich-filled stomach. How could such a magnetic male specimen possibly be…? Forget it, it was too disillusioning to think about.

"The second page is about personal finances and the third one is on entertainment."

This was weird. "Why do we need to fill these out?" She glanced down at the second and third pages and was disconcerted by what she saw. "We don't really need to know whether we secretly order adult movies when we're alone, do we? You know, it's not even legal for you to ask some of this stuff. Maybe all of it."

Cal stopped chewing and looked at her as if she was crazy. As if *she* was the one who had come up with these insane questionnaires. "We're not filling them out about *ourselves*," Cal said.

Now she was thoroughly confused. "I don't understand."

He gave a laugh. "Normally I'd be conducting formal focus groups, but there isn't time for that, so we're going to have to hit the streets and poll people."

"Oh." She felt warmth rise in her cheeks and knew she probably looked like a lobster. An embarrassed lobster. But a *relieved* embarrassed lobster.

This was a good idea he had.

"So when do you want to do this?" she asked him, readying herself to settle in and fine-tune the questions with him.

"Now."

"Now?"

He nodded. "We're going to go out right now, hit at least three or four different neighborhoods and get our own sampling of what women are interested in."

"Okay."

A dimple dented Cal's left cheek. "Though if you want to fill one of these out, you're welcome to."

She shot him a look. "No, thanks."

"I don't think I will, either, though naturally I do appreciate your interest in me."

"I'm not interested in you!" she returned too quickly, and with about a hundred and fifty percent less maturity than she would have liked.

"You just said you thought I should fill out these questionnaires about myself."

"No, I thought that was what *you* were proposing."

"But I told you we were going to interview strangers."

This was exasperating. "Yes, but you said that *after* you said we had to fill them out ourselves."

"Well, we do."

A long beat passed.

"Huh?" Kit asked after a moment.

Cal talked slowly, as if he was talking to a six-year-old. "We're not going to pass them around to people to fill out. That would take forever. We're just going to ask the questions and write the answers down ourselves."

Another beat passed, then Kit said, "You're doing this on purpose, aren't you?"

He raised an eyebrow. "What do you think?"

Her face went warm again and she swatted at him with the clipboard. "I think you're a brat."

"Hey—hang on to that. You're going to need to fill it out." He popped the last bite of sandwich into his mouth and picked up the other clipboard. "Let's go."

"Where do we start?"

"Central Park, of course. I bet there are a bunch of Little League-type games going on. We'll probably find hundreds of women like you."

"Excuse me, Mr. Panagos," Kit said, feigning insult, "but there are *no* women like me out there."

He stopped and looked her over. The look in his eye could have been approval or disapproval, she couldn't tell for sure. But the smile on his face showed one thing: he was, at least, amused. "No, I don't think there are."

Chapter Eight

Cal figured he shouldn't have teased Kit like that, but it had been so long since he'd been around a woman—or *anyone,* actually—he could have fun with. She was easy to bait, that much was evident, but she could also take the joke.

Better still, she *got* the joke.

And she was pretty good at giving back, too. In the cab on the way to the park she'd *almost* had him believing that *Home Life* had once done a series on mothers who were prostitutes while their kids were at school and their husbands were at work.

In the end, she hadn't been able to keep from

laughing, but she *had* given Cal an interesting idea for an article.

It was a hot, sunny Saturday. Not a cloud in the sky, and a light breeze ruffled through the leafy green trees. The park was absolutely full of people, and once there, they had no trouble at all finding fields full of soccer/baseball/T-ball moms and other women who looked to be approximately in *Home Life*'s projected demographic.

"But they are *not* going to talk about all this personal stuff with strangers," Kit said, shaking her head as they slipped down a grassy hill. "In fact, I'm a little afraid someone might call the police on us when we approach them."

"This is New York," Cal said as they walked toward a soccer game surrounded by parents. "People are used to being approached by all kinds of pollsters. Just tell them you work for *Home Life* and you're doing an article."

"Anyone who's ever read *Home Life* would have to be suspicious of these questions if we said they were for that purpose. Let's just tell them we're working for a forthcoming publication from the Monahan Group."

"Perfect."

She was good. He just couldn't deny it. She hadn't exaggerated when she'd sold him on her value that first day. If anything, she'd sold herself short.

They got to the game and split up, Cal going left and Kit going right. He stood for a moment and watched her weave her way through the crowd. People would respond to her. She had a smile that made others feel at ease. An openness that made people want to help her.

Hell, he'd fallen for it himself.

The sun bounced off her deep amber hair as if it was a mirror. She was conspicuously attractive. And the funny thing was, she didn't seem to know it.

That made her even more attractive.

He could have watched her all day, but he had to do the same thing she was doing. He needed to hear from more than just one woman about what it was that women wanted.

The interview process in the park took about an hour. Cal had gotten a few good interviews, but he'd also gotten several looks of fear or concern and three telephone numbers. Not that he'd asked for them. And he certainly wasn't going to call them.

Still, from where he stood, it looked as if Kit was a lot more productive at this than he was, at least so far.

Good thing they were on the same team.

"How'd it go?" he asked her as they met on the path and started walking up toward the street.

She held up a clipboard filled with notes. "Excellent. I have to say, you were right. People were *way* more willing to talk about their private lives than I thought. In all cases, I was more embarrassed than the person telling me about her personal-maintenance issues or mental-health prescriptions."

Cal smiled. She'd done great, just great. Only a couple of days ago he'd been determined to fire her, but now—even though she certainly hadn't done anything to dissuade his concern that she was a distraction—she'd proven herself to be extremely valuable.

"How about you?" she asked, sneaking a peek at his almost-empty sheets.

"Turns out women are a little reluctant to talk to men about their personal issues." Either that or they wanted to dive right into their personal issues, literally.

Kit nodded. "I'm not surprised." They reached the sidewalk and moved into a taxi waiting in the cab lane. "You know what you should do?" she asked suddenly.

"What's that?"

She took his clipboard, saying, "Oh, my God, I can't believe I didn't think of this before."

He looked over her shoulder, trying to read what she was writing. "What are you doing?"

She held up her hand. "Wait a sec."

He sat back against the seat and locked eyes for a second with the driver in the rearview mirror.

He shrugged and the man nodded.

Kit scribbled away like a madwoman during the long drive downtown and across the bridge into Brooklyn. Cal had little to do except look at her and wonder if there was any chance that, with Kit at his side, he might actually be able to make *Home Life* work.

"Here," she said finally, handing him the clipboard. She'd turned all the sheets of paper over and written questions on the backs of them.

And she was flushed with excitement.

"What is this?" he asked, looking over the questions.

"You're going to talk to men," she said proudly.

He snapped his attention to her. "All that time you were writing this down so I could talk to *men?* Why waste the time? Men aren't going to buy the magazine, women are."

"Exactly." She wiggled her eyebrows. Her green eyes were lit as if from within.

Cal felt a strange impulse to kiss her.

So he decided to go with his confusion instead. "I'm not following."

"Those—" she tapped the clipboard "—are all the things women want to know about men but are afraid to ask. If you're looking for a good feature that women will want to read, that's it right there."

He sighed. "What, like *Do you prefer women with makeup or without?* and *Boxers or briefs?* That's been done before."

She smiled and shook her head. "May I refer you to question three?"

He looked down, read it and said, "I'm not going up to some guy and asking him that."

"Women want to know!"

"No way. Make up your own answer."

"Come on," she said. "*You* answer it."

"I'm not answering that question."

She looked very pleased with herself. "Hmm. Sounds like we're pushing out of 'been there, done that' territory."

Damn, she was right.

He looked back at the paper. There wasn't one question he'd feel comfortable walking up to a man on the street and asking. "Let's trade jobs. You ask the men this stuff and I'll talk to women."

"I would, but I don't think men, by and large, would be comfortable talking to a women about this stuff."

"Men wouldn't necessarily be comfortable talking to their doctor about some of this."

"Exactly why it's going to be a killer article for a women's magazine."

The cab pulled up on Tilden Street. Cal had never been so reluctant to leave a cab before, but he knew Kit was right. Having her conduct a modified focus group and him gather information for their first feature article killed two birds with one stone.

They got out of the car and onto the hot, sunny sidewalk. "You're at least going to write the article, right?"

"It might be better coming from you," she said, her eyes dancing. She was totally enjoying his discomfort. "Besides, I have other ideas I need to work on. The moms at the soccer game really enjoyed talking about how hard it is to raise kids and have a life at the same time. I think I'm qualified to write about that."

"Maybe Edith Chamberlain could write it," Cal grumbled.

"Or J. T. Kidman."

"Who?"

She winked and pointed at him. "J. T. Kidman. Or Nom de Plume. Or whatever else you might want to call yourself so your mom doesn't know you're writing an article about all of that."

"I'm not a writer!"

She shrugged. "Desperate times call for desperate measures. I know you're used to the big time, Panagos, but here in the small time we sometimes have to double-park, so to speak."

"You're a pain in the neck, Macy, you know that?"

She laughed. "I haven't had this much fun in ages. If nothing else, you've made this job a whole lot more interesting."

"Yeah, yeah, yeah." He put a hand on her shoulder and guided her up the street to a more crowded area where they could begin to interview people. "Let's just see if we can make the *magazine* a little more interesting, okay?"

"Question ten should do the trick there," she said, then she giggled and rounded the corner before he could grab her and give her the kiss he was trying so hard to resist.

Never in her life had Kit thought of Brooklyn as a romantic place, but when Cal had put his hand on her shoulder and steered her up the street, she had nearly gone faint under the heat of his touch. One more second and she might have turned to him then and there and thrown herself into his arms.

So instead she turned onto Penn Avenue and made some inane comment about "People straight ahead."

As if it was incredibly lucky that they'd managed to find people on the street in Brooklyn on a warm Saturday afternoon.

Kit did not know what was going on with her, but she was finding this…well, there was no other word for it, this *crush* on Cal to be immensely disturbing.

Yes, he was classically handsome. Really attractive. Movie-star gorgeous. But she'd never been shallow. Even in high school she hadn't gone for the cute morons—she'd preferred a more homely guy with brains and a sense of humor.

Of course, Cal had brains and a sense of humor, so that made him double trouble right there.

Still, this was the man who had come to fire her. She'd had to *beg* him to let her keep her job, and even then he'd only committed—not on paper, she'd noticed—to two months.

So was this some sort of weird mutation of Stockholm syndrome she was feeling, where she was desperately attracted to a man who could fire her at any moment?

Or was it something else, maybe perimenopause kicking in and sending her hormones on a ride.

The irony was annoying. Here she was, given the opportunity of a lifetime to speak to women her age and in her stage of life, and she was suddenly like a teenager with a crush.

As they had in Central Park, Cal and Kit had gone in opposite directions when they got into Brooklyn. Her part was easy—she connected with the women she spoke to. A lot of them were going through the same kinds of things she was as a single mother. Even some of the married ones saw their husbands so infrequently that they *felt* like single mothers and struggled with many of the same issues.

Before long Kit felt as if she had everything she needed in order to get started, so she went off in search of Cal.

It wasn't hard to find him. All she needed to do was follow the admiring glances of women on the street and there he was.

He was speaking with a very tall potbellied man in a sleeveless undershirt when Kit got to him.

When she saw the man raise his hand and slap it down on Cal's back, she panicked, thinking he'd ended up talking to the wrong guy and was now going to get the cuss kicked out of him. But it turned out the two were whooping it up like old fraternity brothers.

"Here she is now," Cal said when Kit arrived. The look he flashed her made it clear he wanted to get out of there now.

"Oh, I gotta tell her," the big man said in a deep baritone voice twanging so heavily with the local accent that she could practically taste a Coney dog.

"Bart wants to tell you about his pal Knocker and a deer they found when they went camping one time," Cal said, widening his eyes meaningfully.

She understood. "I'd love to hear it, but we were supposed to be at that meeting forty minutes ago!"

He gaped in mock horror. "It's already, um—"

"After six." She nodded. "We've got to go right away. If we do, we might still catch them at dinner."

Cal turned an apologetic expression on Bart. "The lady says we've got to go."

"Aw, they're always telling us what to do. Hey— put *that* in your newspaper."

"Will do. Thanks again for your time. It's been a blast." He started walking away with Kit, saying, between clenched teeth, "Don't look back. Whatever happens. I don't care if you hear gunfire or Ed McMahon saying he's got your check, just keep walking."

"If Ed McMahon's back there with my check, I'm going."

"If Ed McMahon's back there with your check, I'll double it." He knocked her gently with his arm. "You did good, by the way. Good improvising."

"I have a four-year-old. I have to improvise daily, usually with much tougher subjects than that."

"I bet. You're probably a really cool mom."

"Icy."

With a quick backward glance he turned at the next corner onto a dark, shaded, narrow street.

At his expression of relief, Kit burst out laughing. "Okay, what was that business with Bart all about?"

"You don't want to know. Trust me."

"Sounds interesting."

"Only if gross is the new interesting."

"Ew, he didn't—" She couldn't even finish the sentence. "He and his pal didn't…"

"What?" Cal looked at her. "No. No, nothing like that. Really. It was disgusting but not illegal." He thought for a moment. "At least I don't think it's illegal. Anyway, forget it." They arrived at the next corner and he hailed a cab.

He opened the door for Kit and as she went past him, he said, "Let's not talk about that again, okay?"

She was about to demand that he tell her once and for all exactly what Bart had said, but then she saw the smile on his face and she knew he was pulling her leg. "Very funny."

"Thanks."

He gave the driver the address and they went speeding off into the evening, back toward the city.

It was date night in one of the sexiest cities in the world and Kit was with the most gorgeous man she'd ever met. The shadows were falling across the streets now and it would take a hard woman not to be bowled over by the symbolism.

Fortunately Kit was a hard woman.

Or at least she was going to try to be.

Chapter Nine

Although Kit had half hoped that she might go back to the office with Cal, she knew they'd accomplished everything they were going to that day and they both needed to get to work.

He must have been thinking the same thing, because he got out a couple of blocks from the office and paid the driver to take Kit back to her house so she didn't have to rely on public transportation at this hour of the evening.

Newly inspired by her talks with women that day—

and determined to stop thinking unholy thoughts about Cal—Kit went back to the computer and started writing again.

Diary of a Domestic Goddess
I'll Bring the Dip

As the night wears on, he gets louder and more embarrassing. People look at you, at first with pity, then with thinly veiled intolerance and eventually with overt disgust. And who can blame them, really?

His jokes are incoherent, but he's unstoppable. When you subtly try to get him to pipe down, he asks, in shouted indignation, "What do you mean 'Be quiet'?" Begging doesn't help. Threatening doesn't help. And if you're not careful, you'll push the wrong button and, like a Chatty Cathy doll gone mad, a string of overly personal facts about YOU will come out of his mouth.

The later it gets, the more vulnerable everyone and everything in the room becomes to spilled drinks and personal observations. He loses his footing, is almost guaranteed to spill his drink on your friend's new white carpet and leaves half-consumed cans and bottles ev-

erywhere. And God help anyone who has a noticeable imperfection on their face.

By the end of the night you wonder if you can ever face any of them again, yet you still have the kiss good-night ahead of you. But what can you do? You love him. It's because of you he was there in the first place.

He's your four-year-old son.

And he's absolutely ruining your social life.

Soon friends stop inviting you over or mark "Adults Only" on their invitations. If you were dating him, you'd dump him. But you're not dating him. In fact, you're not dating anyone, thanks to this social sabotage.

Cal looked at the paper in his hand for a long time before laying it on his desk and looking at Kit. "I like it."

"You do?" This was incredible. They were really starting to connect, professionally speaking.

He nodded thoughtfully. "I do."

"See?" She resisted being smug, but it wasn't easy. "I told you I could give you what you were looking for. Women today are struggling with what they thought motherhood was supposed to look like versus what it *really* looks like, and—"

"I meant the title."

She stopped. Her smugness popped like a big water balloon. "What?"

"The title. *Diary of a Domestic Goddess.* I sort of like it. It has a certain nouveau-retro vibe that's playing really well in the marketplace right now."

"The title," Kit repeated.

"Uh-huh."

"That's *all* you liked?"

He stood up. "I've got to go get something to eat. Walk with me."

"What?"

He pointed to his watch. "It's noon. Aren't you hungry? I'm hungry."

"I—" What the heck was going on? Weren't they having an editorial meeting? "Can't you just order in?"

He shook his head. "No. I want to see the stuff. Come on."

It was as if all their camaraderie on Saturday had been a figment of her imagination. She had to win him over all over again, so she went with him, planning to do just that.

They went into the hall and Cal poked the elevator button and turned to Kit. "Can I be honest with you?"

Nothing good ever followed that question. She straightened her back. "Of course."

"You're not going deep enough. You're not opening yourself up enough."

The way he looked at her sent a frisson of energy coursing down her spine. She felt naked before him and he was telling her to show *more*.

The doors to the elevator opened and they got on with a man Kit recognized as a pharmaceutical salesman for the doctors' offices upstairs and a middle-aged woman with shoe-polish-black hair whom she'd passed in the lobby for five years but didn't know the first thing about.

"You need to be more open," Cal went on as the elevator doors crept closed at a snail's pace.

"How much more open can I be?" she asked quietly, glancing at the other people around them to see if they were paying attention. They didn't appear to be. "There wasn't anything I *avoided* saying."

"But you only told half the story," Cal said in a voice that might as well have been over a microphone.

The elevator slowed to a halt and the doors opened. Two more women got on, and Kit noticed that both of them looked at Cal appreciatively.

"You've come close to the mark but you stopped short," Cal explained. "You played it safe. For instance, you alluded to how hard it is to date, but you

didn't say anything more about it. Yet you're talking about being a single mother. That raises obvious
questions. How do you date with a kid around? What
happens when you have a guy sleep over or you
want to stay over at his place?"

Her cheeks burned, but she refused to be the
ninny who asked if he could lower his voice or talk
to her about this in private. "That's not really the
thrust of my piece, though."

The pharmaceutical salesman cleared his throat.

Her cheeks burned more. "Dating, I mean. To ex-
pound upon that would have been irrelevant."

"No, it wouldn't have. That's what I'm trying to
say. Anyone can *tell* you it's hard to be a single parent and date. Even *I* could have told you that and I
haven't been near a kid in years."

"A*men*," one of the women said, nodding.

"See?" Cal pointed to her with his thumb.
"Thank you, ma'am. Now wouldn't you rather see
someone tell the truth about that instead of sugar-
coating it with all kinds of impractical Stepford-
wife suggestions?"

"Uh-huh," the woman said, nodding broadly.
"Don't tell me to join a church group when I can't even
get my butt out of bed before noon on the weekend."

"What about those matchmaking sites online?"
her companion added. "It's a huge gamble, and you

can't tell from the pictures or the profiles who's a nice guy and who's a weirdo still living in his mother's basement."

Cal nodded, as if they were preaching to the choir. "Exactly my point. Thank you, ladies."

The elevator stopped at long last and everyone got out.

"I want a writer who's ready to *show* it all," Cal said to her. "Especially the hard parts."

"I see."

They stepped outside onto the sunny, hot sidewalk, which was bustling with so much activity it was more crowded than the elevator. "Young women today lay it on the line when they talk to each other. They'll say it all, they'll tell it all."

"Young women," she repeated coolly. Next was he going to tell her that all of her work on Saturday was for nothing because she hadn't talked to women young enough? What did he see as the new face of this magazine—Katie Holmes? "What's your definition of young?"

He stopped and turned to her. "How old are you?"

She shook her head, looking him dead in the eye. "It's against the law for you to ask me that."

He looked her over and added two years to his guess, just to goad her. "Thirty-eight?"

She took a sharp breath inward. "No."

He shifted his weight, ignoring the irritated looks of passersby who now had to walk around him. "Is it against the law for me to ask how long you've been divorced?"

"Cal, what could that *possibly* have to do with my job performance?"

"If it has to do with your personal point of view and you're writing point-of-view columns, I'd say quite a bit."

"I'm a professional." She glanced behind Cal as a man dressed as a taco walked up, handing out flyers. "I can write what's called for," she said, taking the menu for Tippy's Taco House.

He let out a long, tight breath. "Listen, Kit—"

She was jostled when someone shouted something about hot beef injections and shoved the taco guy against her, sending her slamming hard against Cal's chest.

"Hey," Cal put his hands on her shoulders gently, drawing her back. "Are you okay?"

She nodded, still trying to catch her breath. "Fine."

Tippy the Taco, however, was still lying on the ground, and she reached a hand out to help him up while throngs of people walked by without acknowledgement.

Cal put a hand out, too, and hoisted the heavy costumed man to his feet.

"Thanks, man," the taco said in a weary voice and walked away.

Kit and Cal looked at each other and laughed.

They began walking again and Cal said, "Look, Kit. You did a great job on Saturday. I know you've got it in you. Hell, your eleventh question for men proves that. Now ask yourself some of the same questions. Or at least use the same level of honesty. Go back to your drawing board and give me something more relevant. Something interesting."

"Interesting to you or to the people we talked to over the weekend?"

"To both of us."

She shook her head. "Given what I know of you so far, I don't think what's interesting to you is necessarily going to be interesting to women twenty-four to forty."

They turned the corner and stopped in front of Dingo's Deli. "Then you're going to have to write something that's interesting to me," he said. "Because I'm the one you have to impress first."

She looked at him for a long, hard moment. Her green eyes seemed to turn a dark, mossy gray, though that had to be his imagination. "You know, Cal," she said at last. "Unless you give up a little bit of this control, I don't think this is going to work."

This wasn't what he'd expected. "You don't think *what* is going to work?"

"You. Me. This." She gestured between the two of them. "*We* clearly aren't going to work well together."

"Are you…breaking up with me?" He couldn't believe it. No one had ever dumped him. *Especially* not in a business situation.

Worse, he didn't want her to go.

Not that he couldn't do without her—Cal Panagos had never counted on anyone but himself. It was just that…he'd grown accustomed to her face, as the old song went.

"No, I'm just saying that if you want this to work, you might need to back off. Trust me a little bit, even if it's counterintuitive for you. Because I'm right."

"You are?"

She nodded. "I absolutely am. You've got a great resource in me, a conduit directly to your target demographic, but you won't use it. You're not willing to listen to the one person in your orbit who's willing and able to give you advice on how to touch them. Touch *us*," she corrected, inadvertently putting ideas in his head that were decidedly unprofessional.

He should have just let her go. Let her walk away and never come back, leaving him to his pastrami on pumpernickel and his terrible magazine. His life would have been a whole lot easier if she did, he could tell that with complete certainty already.

"I'm hungry," he said. "I can't have this kind of conversation on an empty stomach."

She glanced at the deli door. "You don't want to eat anything from there."

"Yes, I do."

"The salad guy has allergies and sneezes *constantly*," she said. "And without being careful about the food."

"Oh." He looked around. "What do you suggest?"

"Carmels."

"Where's that?"

"Six blocks west. I usually call my order in."

"Why didn't you say that to begin with?" He shook his head. "You've got the number?"

She looked as if she was trying not to smile. "In my office."

"Let's go." They walked back to the office at a much faster clip than they'd left.

"See how much you need me?" Kit teased as she hurried along behind him into the building and through the lobby.

He punched the elevator button and turned to her. "You or Zagat restaurant reviews?"

They stepped onto the elevator.

This time Kit didn't care who was on there with them.

"If you need my help with something as basic as the pastrami, how in the world do you expect to satisfy all those women without my advice?"

A clean-cut young man who was on the elevator with them reached out and pushed a button to stop at the next floor and got off, throwing a disapproving glance over his shoulder at them.

"Have you ever been to a Parents Alone meeting?" Cal asked Kit.

"I'm not sure it's legal for you—"

"*Damn* it, Kit, could you answer one question about yourself without an argument?"

She raised her eyebrows. "Okay. Thirty-six."

He hesitated. She'd been to thirty-six meetings? She'd kept track? That almost seemed consistent with her personality...but then he realized what she was saying. "Your age. Thirty-six."

She nodded coolly, then smiled and stepped off the elevator on the *Home Life* floor. "Very good. And to answer your other question, a couple."

He tried to remember what else she'd refused to answer. "You've been divorced a couple of years?"

"No, I've been to a couple of Parents Alone meetings. How long I've been divorced is none of your business."

She'd thrown him completely off balance for a minute.

Again.

He *hated* that.

He tried to remember where he'd been going so

he could put the conversation back on track. "I went to a Parents Alone meeting the other night to see what they talked about, to find out what their concerns were—"

"Did you tell them you weren't a single parent?"

"Of course not." He threw open the door to the offices. "Anyway—"

"Wait a minute, that's just wrong," Kit said, catching the door. "You can't go *spy* at a Parents Alone meeting. That's against the spirit of everything they stand for."

"Yeah, well, add it to the list of things you're going to sue me for." He didn't have a lot of patience for an ethics discussion right now.

He was starving. He needed to tell his secretary to call in the order.

"Anyway," he said to Kit as they walked side by side back to his office, "there was a lot of talk about how hard it was to date but how much everyone wanted to get laid." He saw an objection forming like storm clouds in her expression and held his hands up. "Hey, their words, not mine."

"That's *not* indicative of the feelings of modern mothers across the nation."

"That's what I thought. So I went to a PTA meeting at the elementary school near my parents' house in Jersey and I hung around afterward listening." He shook his head. "It's truly amazing what women will say out loud, even with strangers around. Turns out, they had the same frustrations as the singles. In graphic detail. The upshot is that no one's getting any action, except for one guy who refused to let his wife get a kitten until she—"

"Okay, got it." Kit splayed her arms. "You want something *salacious.*"

He shrugged. "Well, yeah. As long as it's the truth." They stopped in front of his door and his eyes traveled up the length of her again. He couldn't help it. "You up for it?"

"Are you?"

"Always." He wasn't sure. He wasn't sure at all.

He called to his secretary to order his sandwich and raised an eyebrow at Kit. She added her order and they went back into his office.

Only this time there was a distinct shift in power.

"Then you've got it." She sat and crossed her legs. "But I don't want you complaining later that I went too far."

There was definitely a shift in power. He just couldn't let her know it. "I can assure you, I have never accused a woman of going too far."

She looked into his eyes and something sizzled between them.

"For instance," he said, then cleared his throat.

"That question on the poll we conducted. About escorts. Did you know that one in twenty businesswomen in New York has at some point hired an escort?"

"Five percent?" She couldn't believe that. "No way."

"And half of them have had sex with them."

"Really?"

He nodded. "I want you to check this out. I know of three women who would be willing to talk to you about it, and maybe one of them could write the article. Not about the tragedy of it, you understand."

"No, about the *practicality*." Kit was fascinated.

"Exactly."

They were back on track.

"So get on that. I want it frank without being too obvious. Provocative without being self-conscious. I want to hear about the freedom of it, the reasons it works sometimes, since we all can imagine why it wouldn't work."

She nodded, making mental notes.

"I want excitement," Cal went on. "I want sex—"

"Can we stay on the topic of the magazine?" She raised an eyebrow.

It might have been her imagination, but it looked as if Cal's cheeks went slightly red. "Very cute," he said. "This is not about my life."

"If you say so." Of course she was teasing, but she found his uncomfortable reaction interesting.

"My sex life has nothing to do with any of this."

"Of course not." She was having fun with this newfound modesty she'd discovered in Cal.

"And for the record, I've got no complaints."

"Ah, but have you *heard* any complaints?"

He leveled a cool blue gaze on her. "None."

The energy between them shifted abruptly.

It was clear that Cal Panagos had a lot of sexual confidence. Kit went from lighthearted to breathless in a split second, then tried to put the entire prospect out of her mind before she said something stupid or regrettable.

But before she got the chance to change the subject, Cal added, "Do you need references?"

She gave him a look.

"A demonstration?"

Kit tried to make her look withering, but inside nothing was withering. In fact, her entire body was springing to life in a disconcerting way. "No, thanks." She made a show of sighing wearily, even though inside her nerves were stretched as tight as a drum. "You're not easy to work with, are you?"

He gave a short laugh. "Depends who you ask."

The door opened and a brawny man in a sweaty T-shirt and jeans tightly cinched by a tool belt came in, looking around like a lost tourist. "Oh. Sorry to interrupt. I need to do some measurements."

Cal gestured for him to come in, and the man took a tape measure out of his tool belt and began making measurements and jotting notes on a small pad.

"What's that about?" Kit asked.

"Just doing a little bit of remodeling. Freshen the place up some. I swear it smells like a rest home in here."

Kit could only nod. Lila Harper had made many lavender sachets and put them into the filing cabinets, swearing it would keep the documents fresh and free of whatever bugs she imagined would come in and eat paper documents.

Those combined with the strong liniment smell that always surrounded certain employees made for a truly disagreeable combination.

Everyone had hated the smell and Kit had carefully gone around and removed the offending items without Lila finding out, but there had been so many—or they were just so strongly scented—that Cal was right, the place still smelled of them.

"Yous want dis window widened?" the worker asked, swiping his forearm across his nose.

Cal turned to him. "No, you're just replacing the windows."

Not a cheap proposition, Kit thought. The money

could be better spent on new talent for the magazine, but she wasn't about to say so and risk incurring Cal's wrath.

Besides, he had a track record that proved he did his job pretty damn well. Who was she to question him on something as stupid as remodeling the office?

She was qualified to tell him what women wanted—though she figured he probably had a lot of experience in that department, too—but other than that, she'd let him make the rules.

At least for a while.

Chapter Ten

That night Kit stayed up late, first looking over the preliminary articles Cal had asked the new writers to forward to her for editing, then culling articles from all over the Internet, finding new voices she thought would be perfect for the new *Home Life.*

She e-mailed prime examples to Cal and waited all the next morning for what she expected to be an enthusiastic response.

"Did he like them?" Jo asked when she called for the second time.

"I haven't heard from him," Kit said.

"Then *ask* him."

"No, I don't want to look too eager." She wasn't actually that worried about his reaction to her work at this point, but if he figured out she went weak in the knees around him, it would be all over for her.

Jo gave an exasperated sigh. "Well, *aren't* you eager?"

"I can't afford to be," Kit said, meaning it more than she could say. "If he sees that kind of weakness, he'll pounce. Then it'll be all over."

"For Pete's sake, Kit, don't be so wimpy. You don't need to be afraid of him."

"I'm not *afraid*—" She caught a glimpse of Cal in the hallway, headed for her office. "He's coming! I've got to go!" She hung the phone up and started clicking on her computer keyboard just as he walked in.

"Kit?" He tapped gently on the open door.

She looked up and feigned surprise. "Oh! Cal! Please—" she gestured at the chair in front of her desk "—have a seat." She sat back and waited for him to tell her how brilliant he thought she was and how in sync with the American woman he now saw she was.

"Actually I was just trying to remember the name of that Italian place you were telling me about yesterday. The one with the great tuna carpaccio?"

"Carrese's?"

He snapped. "Carrese's! I kept thinking Cucinca." He shook his head. "Thanks, Kit. By the way, did you edit those articles yet?"

"I'm almost finished."

"It's a good start, huh?" He looked pleased with himself. "I didn't think we'd be able to get this far this soon." He gave her the thumbs-up and started to leave.

She swallowed her pride and cleared her throat. "Cal?"

He poked his head back in. "Yup?"

"Did you get a chance to look over the stuff I sent *you?*"

"Oh, yeah." He stepped in. "That wasn't quite what I was looking for, but thanks."

"Are you kidding me?"

He leaned against her door frame and said, "Not at all."

She took a steadying breath. "We need to talk about this. We're still hiring. If you want me to do my job, we have to be on the same page, so to speak, as far as who you want to hire."

"You're absolutely right. Meet me in my office in say—" he glanced at his watch "—twenty minutes?"

"Fine."

"Want anything from Carrese's?"

A bottle or two of Chianti, she thought drily. "No. Thanks."

Twenty minutes later on the dot she was back in his office, watching him eat his tuna carpaccio and wishing she'd ordered one herself.

But that wasn't the point of the meeting. "Okay," Kit said. "You've obviously got something specific in mind that you want. Something I haven't touched on yet. Do you want to tell me what it is or should I keep asking?"

"Glad you asked." Cal gave a quick, wicked pirate smile, opened the small refrigerator in the right panel of his desk, took out a cold bottled water and held it out to her in offer.

She shook her head.

He kicked the door closed and twisted the cap off the bottle. "What would you think about going undercover in an honest-to-God harem?"

She looked at him. "You're joking, right?"

He shook his head. "I've got an in. Don't ask how. But if I can get a beautiful woman who's willing to take the chance, she can go in and find out what really goes on."

"I don't speak the language. I don't even know what the language is, but unless it's English, I don't speak it."

"It's an American harem. For a Saudi prince."

"Seriously?"

He nodded.

"That's interesting. I'm not doing it, of course. I can't imagine telling my son I have to go away for a few weeks to play wife to some multiwived prince, but we should get someone in there."

"That's what I'm thinking. The sooner the better. I don't know how long the opportunity will last."

"I'll get on it." She hesitated. "You weren't actually thinking I'd say yes to that, were you?"

He gave a laugh. "I'm still getting to know you, Kit. This is so much more interesting than asking what your favorite color is or what kind of tree you'd be."

She didn't have time to come up with a clever comeback before there was a knock at the door.

"Mr. Pingus?" A young blond woman poked her head inside the door.

Kit shot him a questioning look.

"She's a temp," he said quickly, then added so quietly that only Kit heard, "Very temp." He looked at the girl who was still standing in the doorway. "What is it?"

"Um." She blushed. "Miss Crispy is here to see you."

"Send her in."

Kit started to get up. "I'm going to go make some calls about that assignment we were just talking about."

"No, stay. Diana Kreskin is here to talk about doing a fashion column. You should be here for this."

"Okay. Good." Kit settled back in her seat, glad with the knowledge that he was at least taking her work here seriously enough to keep her involved in the hiring process. "What happened to the secretary you had the other day?" she asked him while they waited for Diana Kreskin, whoever she was.

Cal lifted a shoulder in half a shrug. "Monahan took her back. He's feeling proprietary about my old staff."

"Oh." That was weird.

"Now next week I have interviews set up for Monday and Tuesday," Cal went on. "You're welcome to be here for them, especially since you should be pulling in your own candidates."

"By Monday?" It was already Tuesday. She'd have to place an ad immediately. "I'll get something together."

The door opened again and a knockout of a woman waltzed in. She was built like a brick house—and showcased it by wearing a short, short skirt and almost ridiculously high heels—with long auburn hair and eyes the bright green of colored contacts. "Cal!" she exclaimed, holding out both her hands and coming toward him.

He stood up and accepted her embrace. "Good to

see you again, Diana. This is Kit Macy, our managing editor."

Diana gave her the briefest glance. "So nice to meet you," she said without an iota of sincerity. "Cal, baby, tell me what we're doing here. You're starting a new magazine?"

He gave a nod. "That's the size of it."

"Well, if anyone is qualified to do that, it's you. And you know no one is better for your fashion trends column than *I* am." She sat down and crossed her long, thin legs.

Kit noticed her Pinelli shoes squeaked with the movement.

"London, Milan, Paris, the world is my playground," Diana went on. She raised an eyebrow at Cal. "Maybe you'd like to come play with me?"

Kit winced inwardly.

Cal must have, too, because he shot an uncomfortable glance in Kit's direction before coolly saying to Diana, "Nice offer, but I don't have much time to play these days."

The interview seemed to go on forever, with Diana flirting mercilessly with Cal throughout and acting as if Kit were simply a strangely unwieldy piece of furniture next to her. She glanced at Kit occasionally but didn't make eye contact and, in fact, she didn't appear to register Kit as another employee of the magazine—or, in fact, *person in the room*—at all.

When it was finally over, Cal thanked Diana for coming by and promised to get back to her soon.

After Diana's exit, he turned to Kit and said, "I think she'll be an excellent addition here."

Kit's jaw dropped. "Are you joking?"

"Not at all. Are you?" He frowned and enumerated what he obviously considered Diana's irresistible assets. "She's gorgeous, she's confident, she's well-traveled and she knows her stuff."

Kit gave a halfhearted nod, unable to resist being catty. "Unless her stuff is fashion."

Cal sat up straight. "What are you talking about? She's a fashion expert. Just look how she dresses."

"That's what you're judging her on? How she looked today?"

"She always looks fine."

Though Kit could have questioned him on what he meant by both *always* and *fine* and whether or not clothes were necessarily involved in her supposedly fantastic looks. But she thought better of it. "First of all, she was wearing fake Pinellis—"

"What the hell are fake Pinellis?"

"Her shoes. They squeaked when she walked. Real Pinellis would never do that." She felt catty, but she didn't care. "Nor would they bleed black onto her stockings."

"Okay, so what if they were fakes?"

"No fashion editor worth her salt would be caught dead in corner-vendor fakes, whether they're shoes, bags, whatever. But more to the point, we don't *need* a fashion editor at all."

Cal leaned back again and gave a heavy sigh. "How do you figure that? It's a women's magazine. Isn't that a staple of the genre?"

"All the women's magazines have pages and pages of uninspiring fashion stuff," Kit said, without pointing out that until recently *Home Life* had forgone even that in favor of Lila Harper's "Sewing Corner." "Maybe we should just skip that altogether in favor of more substantial, meaningful articles."

He lifted an eyebrow. "Like how to make Halloween costumes out of household objects?"

Her cheeks burned. "The format has changed, remember?"

He smiled.

Her cheeks burned still more. "What I was trying to say," she continued, "was that if you want the magazine to be different, then make it *different*. Don't do the same things every other women's publication does and don't do things just because you think that's what a women's publication *should* do."

He frowned and tapped his pen on the desk thoughtfully. "You may be right."

That took her by surprise. "Did I hear correctly?"

"Well, you may be *partially* right. No obligatory articles. No same old, same old. I'm thinking guest experts—the designers themselves—writing the articles. Better still, celebrity chefs who want to hawk their new books anyway. It's publicity for them, it's variety for us. Cross promotion. It works for everyone."

"Okay…"

"Good thinking, Kit."

Was this a test? Was he trying to see if she'd take credit for an idea that he had just run with himself? "All I suggested was that we avoid doing the same stuff everyone else is."

He gave a satisfied nod. "And you were exactly right about that, Kit."

Something was up. She still felt as though he was testing her. Another shoe was going to drop, she knew it. And it would probably be a spike-heeled Pinelli original. "What are you up to?"

"I'm going to do a fashion column," he said. "But you've got me thinking. No models. That is, no thin, waifish fashion models wearing clothes no real person would be caught dead in. Real people. Real ideas." He looked thoughtful. "This might just work."

Chapter Eleven

Diary of a Domestic Goddess
"It's a Living"

> The other day I drove eight miles each way to
> the Save-Lots when I saw in the Sunday flyer
> that the supersize laundry detergent I had just
> bought had a five-dollar-off coupon. Five dol-
> lars! I thought, complete with the exclamation
> point. Five dollars! The ten-year-old whose
> allowance was two dollars a week is still deep
> within me, so on some level five dollars still

sounds like a fortune to my ears. I went, I got my refund, I was triumphant.

Until I thought about the mileage I get in my car. And the fact that gas is at the moment almost two bucks a gallon in my town. That right there took my profit down to three bucks. The Diet Coke I added on my trip was another one-oh-nine. Fruit snacks for my boy? Ninety-nine cents. Profit's down to ninety-two cents. Wear and tear on the car? Well, let's not go crazy, but the point is the price a lot of us pay for working at home is feeling broke all the time.

So I'm looking into cottage industry—ways to supplement my income from home. Twenty years ago, tons of women supplemented the family income with door-to-door sales, but in the 80s and 90s we were way too busy for that kind of quaint nonsense. Well, the quaint nonsense is back but it isn't so quaint anymore.

Take Lizzy B. She sold Tupperware for a while and made a pretty decent living. Good stuff, customers loved it. But the well ran dry. Everyone's cereal was neatly put away and they didn't need anymore airtight containers. So Lizzy switched to Creative Chef parties. Give 'em something to put in the plastic containers. Same deal. They bought until there was nothing left to buy. Now she does Passion Princess parties, and the money keeps rolling in. Because, it seems, there is no end to the imagination of the Passion Toys creators—or that of their customers…

"...I have a door prize for each one of you just for showing up tonight." Lizzy Berkower walked from one stretch-jean-clad harried mother to the next, handing out lipsticks. "It's just my way of thanking you and encouraging you to remember me."

Kit examined the lipstick tube. It had Lizzy's name, telephone number and e-mail address—FunwithLizzy@passionprincesses.com—written in glamorous script across the lid. She opened it and twisted the bottom to see what color it was, apparently at the same time as the rest of the party guests because everyone started to laugh at once.

The lipstick was shaped like a part of the male anatomy.

"Pretty hard to forget, huh?" Lizzy smiled.

"Do you have this in a paler pink?" an older woman, the mother of one of the Stretch-Jean Mommies, asked.

"You can order it in just about any color," Lizzy said, taking out a stack of catalogs and asking the party hostess to pass them along. "But I am conducting a raffle tonight for a set of ten, so be sure to fill in the profile sheet I gave you when you got here. That's where the drawing will come through."

"Just watch," the older woman said to her daughter. "I'll win, and when I go home this will be the first time they search my luggage at the airport."

Everyone laughed.

"This is a great color," Jo said, smudging the pinkish red penis along her lips with admittedly impressive results. "Does it come in a, you know, *normal* shape?"

"What's normal?" Lizzy asked with a coy smile. "But, no, that's the only shape I have. At least in that particular shade."

Kit's mind reeled at the other possible shapes she might have in other colors.

"Now I'm going to show you a lot of things tonight," Lizzy continued when the laughter died down. "Then I'm going to ask each one of you into the kitchen to order their Passion Princess products privately. That way, you can order or not order or just talk about the weather, without anyone knowing. If you order, your items will arrive in a brown paper package with my own return address, so you can rest assured that your transaction will be completely private."

Kit made a mental note of the relief she saw on faces around the room.

"So let's get started!" Lizzy pulled out a Mary Poppinsish carpetbag and proceeded to produce one bizarre battery-operated thing after another.

The presentation was fascinating. Kit found herself dying to see what happened by the end. These were women from a normal neighborhood. Some of them were on the PTA board of the local elementary school.

Real women.

Her audience exactly.

"My husband is already ticked off that we hardly ever do it," one woman said after they'd seen several of Lizzy's wares. "If I gave what little energy I had to plastic and rubber, he'd disown me."

"The idea is that you give *him* the plastic and rubber so *he* can use it on you," Lizzy said. "How many of us would appreciate not having to fake it every once in a while, eh?"

Everyone laughed again. Lizzy knew her audience. Lizzy knew Kit's audience.

"Now," Lizzy said, opening her bag. "Let me introduce you to one of my most popular items." She pulled out a toothpaste-shaped tube. "This is super-numbing anesthetic Anu-Glide. And you are going to thank me for this."

Her announcement was met by stunned silence.

"Er...I'm not sure that's my kind of thing," one woman said.

"Oh, yes it is. Believe me." Lizzy waited a beat before continuing. "You put a little of this on your eyebrows before plucking and you don't feel a *thing*."

Everyone burst into laughter and applause.

She smiled. "I'm sorry, I can never resist the looks of horror on most guests' faces when I first mention the Anu-Glide."

As the evening wore on, the champagne flowed and the oysters Rockefeller disappeared. So did the party guests one by one into the kitchen. Some took longer than others, but almost all of them had guilty smiles on their faces when they came back out.

When it was Kit's turn, she was almost embarrassed not to order something. "I'm actually here because I'm doing an article on new ways to make money on your own time," she explained to Lizzy as she sat down at the tile-top table with apples painted on the corners.

Lizzy smiled. "Jo told me. That's fine. I'm glad to help any way I can. So what did you think?"

"I thought I was a prude first-class. But then I began to see that this was a great way for these women—well, all of us—to talk about what's really

going on in our lives. Or not going on in our lives."
She smiled. "This was a bonding experience more
than a shopping experience."

Lizzy patted a good-size stack of order sheets. "Fortunately for me, it was both. But you're right, the thing
that works about it is the way it brings people together.
At first they're embarrassed. And giggly. But usually
by the time the Bottom Buster comes out, people are
really opening up and talking about their issues."

The Bottom Buster was a pair of sexy-looking underpants that possessed the power to whittle one's
hips as much as two inches and hock up sagging
flesh. There had been great excitement in the room
when Lizzy had introduced that little miracle.

"Do you have any questions?" Lizzy asked. "I'd
be glad to help you with your article however I can."

Kit moved on to her prepared questions. "If you
don't mind my asking, approximately how much do
you make doing these parties? More than you would
at an administrative desk job?"

"Last year I made eighty-four grand," Lizzy said,
and before Kit could gasp she added, "That was after
taxes, of course."

Kit let out an astonished breath. "What do you attribute that to? I mean, that's a lot of sales, isn't it?
These things are clearly hot items, but you're not the
only source."

Lizzy nodded. "No, but I'm a source my clients can trust. They know they're not going to end up on some strange mailing list when they buy from me and that their lingerie size will be held in the strictest confidence. But also, we sell a lot more than just the fun, risqué stuff. For instance, we have pads that can be placed outside a bedroom door and sound a small alarm to warn parents when their children are about to walk in. People appreciate it when you address their concerns that way and solve them."

"Aha." Kit made a note on her pad.

"Interested?" Lizzy asked with a keen eye.

"In the alarm pads?" Kit laughed. "No need for that. Except maybe outside my front door, as an intruder alert. Tonight I'm in this for the research. Though I would like a price on the Bottom Busters before I go."

They spent a few minutes chatting about how Lizzy came to work for Passion Princess from a teaching job at a middle school and how she felt it was working out for her. She gave Kit some excellent information, but at the same time Kit's mind was filled with Cal Panagos. And how he probably didn't need to use any of these accessories to please a woman. There was just something about the way he looked at Kit, the way he moved, even the way he smiled, that made her absolutely sure he was amazing in bed.

It was stupid how she could be persuaded to fantasy by a fabulous face and buff body even as the soul inside was only interested in the bottom line.

Not hers, but the magazine's.

"I'll keep you in mind," Kit promised. "If I ever have a date again." She paused, thinking the point of a vibrator was to be your own date. She was glad Lizzy didn't point that out in hopes of making a sale.

Instead she nodded sympathetically. "I hear that a lot." She lowered her voice and asked, "Have you tried going to makemeamatch.com?"

"No." Kit smiled but wondered how desperate she looked. "I'm not…in that place right now."

Like any good salesperson, Lizzy was too tactful to push. "Just keep it in mind," she said. "I've known a lot of people who had good luck there. It's better than being alone." She opened a catalog. "But if you *are* alone, you might be interested in a little number I have here on page twenty-three…."

By Wednesday afternoon, not twenty-four hours after Kit had left the *Home Life* building, the office was well on its way to becoming completely unrecognizable.

Even from outside she could hear the sound of buzz saws inside as she picked her way past contractors' trucks to get to the front door. In the halls the smell of sawdust and paint was prevalent. When she opened the door to the office, she was surprised to see a chrome desk where a big cherrywood one had sat for five decades. There was a young redhead seated behind it with a telephone headset on. Behind her, where the wall had once been carved with the *Home Life* logo, there was a splashy, colorful new logo for *Real Life*.

It was perfect.

"May I help you?" the redhead asked her.

"Yes, where's Cal?"

"I beg your pardon?"

"Kit!" Finally a familiar face, if only barely. Cal Panagos came to her from the direction of what had once been the copy room. Who knew what it was now? "What do you think of the new name?" He gestured toward the logo on the wall behind the receptionist.

"I think it's perfect."

He gave a genuinely happy smile. "Me, too. Real ideas for real women. And it's all thanks to you. You've really helped guide this into place."

She felt her face flush.

A workman fired up a sander about five feet away from them and the noise blasted over the rest of Kit's reply.

Cal put a hand on her shoulder and shouted, "Come to my office!" He was no longer using the empty office he'd occupied yesterday when he'd met with Kit. Instead he led the way down the hall—still untouched and mercifully familiar—to what used to be Ebbit Markham's large corner office.

All of the things that had made it Ebbit's own space, the photo of Connie on his desk and the hideous fish mounted on the wall, were gone. It was an empty shell, completely unfamiliar apart from the view out the window. At least Cal couldn't change that, Kit thought, though she wouldn't have bet money on it.

"Have a seat," Cal said, gesturing vaguely as he sat behind a spare, modern wood desk.

Kit looked around at the otherwise empty room. "On the floor?"

"Oh, hell, I'm sorry." He slapped his hand on an intercom on his desk. "Penny, could you find a chair and bring it in here for Ms. Macy?"

"Sure thing," a woman's voice returned with the slightest hint of a British accent.

"Penny?"

"My new secretary."

"Got rid of the temp, huh?"

"She was awful." He leaned back. "Now. We need to talk about your column. Specifically what you're doing next."

"Next?" She raised her eyebrows. "Does that mean you like my latest work?"

He leveled a gaze on her. "It was…intriguing."

A shiver ran through her. She thought of several parts of the article that she had been worried about showing to him. Had the part about Stretch-Jean Mommies made him look at her differently?

If so, was that a good thing?

"Thanks," she said a little uncertainly.

"Tell me," he went on, the expression in his eyes shifting slightly. "Did you buy anything?"

She was puzzled. "What do you mean?"

He held up the article. "At the party. Did you buy anything?"

The way he asked, and the way he looked at her when he asked, made her realize for the first time that there was more at work here than just…work.

And despite all the reasons she shouldn't be intrigued by that idea—not least of which was how a romantic relationship would fit into her life with Johnny—she couldn't help the thrill it gave her.

Chapter Twelve

She smiled cryptically. "You can't ask me that."

"You're always saying that to me."

"That's because you're so nosy."

He rolled his eyes. "In most circles it would be considered normal curiosity."

"Are you interested in making some purchases for yourself?" she asked him.

He gave her a long look that sent unexpected shivers down her spine. Then, with just the slightest smile playing at the corner of his mouth, he said, "Now *that* is an inappropriate question."

She smiled. "Tit for tat."

He looked at her evenly, just the slightest tug at the corner of his mouth suggesting a smile. "Interesting choice of words. What exactly is *tat?*"

"You'll have to go to one of the parties and find out for yourself," she fired back.

"Will you come with me?"

Again something sizzled between them. Something Kit wasn't expecting.

"To a party?"

His hesitation was long and deliberate. "Wherever you like," he said at last.

Her breath caught in her throat. She honestly wasn't sure if he was issuing double entendres or if it was her own inappropriate thinking that had her hearing them when they weren't there.

She'd been losing the battle of her attraction to him lately, so the latter seemed possible.

"I'm not sure if we're talking about business or pleasure at this point," she said.

He shrugged. "Pleasure is serious business." The moment lingered, with questions unasked and unanswered, until he added, "As you've shown right here in your article."

She swallowed. "Like most of these things, I believe it depends upon your perspective."

"You sound like quite the expert."

She smiled wanly. "I always got good marks for paying attention in school."

"I'm not surprised. That's why I was wondering if you just listened to this woman or if you decided to learn more about the products yourself."

"You can learn plenty just by listening."

He shrugged.

"But I guess that's not quite your style. You're the kind of man who seems more…self-taught." She was having more fun with this than she should.

He smiled and looked down, shaking his head. "I've had to do my share of self-teaching, that's for sure."

Kit cleared her throat. "I'm sorry to hear it."

Were they about to share a moment? Was the great Cal Panagos going to confide what made him tick, what drove him, what had compelled him to become the youngest editor in chief of *Sporting World?*

"So what did you buy?"

Moment over. Opportunity passed.

She wished she'd had a clever reply to that, but instead she fell back on what she'd already said. "If you're interested for your own purposes, I can refer you to Lizzy. But we're here to talk about business, and whether or not *I* purchased something in no way pertains to my *work.*"

"Of course it does."

"Really? What is it you think I do?"

He leveled a cool blue gaze on her for a moment before saying, "You do a lot of things I wasn't quite expecting."

God, he was attractive sometimes.

She was really going to have to try not to think about that.

"I told you I was value-added. Two for the price of one and all that." She looked at him closely to find some sort of flaw she could focus on rather than the blue, blue eyes and the sensual curve of his mouth.

"I didn't say you were doing *good* things." He kept a straight face, but it was clear that he was amused.

Kit rolled her eyes. Clearly she would never be able to outrepartee a master. The real danger, though, was that she was finding his wit a little too attractive. "All right, all right, keep it moving. Are you going to use the article or not?"

"Yes, I'm going to use it. In fact—" he leaned back in his leather chair and it squeaked slightly "—I'm putting you on the cover."

She had a sudden vision of herself on the cover, perhaps superimposed on the body of Pamela Anderson holding a Passion Princess product, with some obnoxious shout line like *Sex: Single Moms are Doing it for Themselves.*

"The article shout line, I mean," he clarified. "I'm thinking something like—" he squinted into the distance as if reading a faraway billboard *"—Selling Sex to Feed the Family."* He continued to look at the imaginary billboard, then frowned and shook his head. "Not that. But something like that. What do you think?"

"It's a grabber."

He pointed at her. "And that is exactly what we want."

There was a buzz from a box on his desk and the redheaded secretary's voice said, "Mr. Panagos, Ed Lindsey from Toronto Printing is on line one."

He picked up the receiver and held his hand up to Kit. "Cal Panagos." He listened for a minute or two, his expression growing darker with every passing second. Finally he said, "We can't afford that kind of delay."

Kit's stomach clenched. This mattered to her. The printing deadline was incredibly important. Even a small delay could be an enormous problem with the time frame Cal had given her in order to succeed.

Cal sat up, his back ramrod straight. "We can have the copy for you within two weeks," he said, his voice as cool as ever, even though Kit knew that having an entire magazine's worth of copy when they didn't even have a full staff of writers was nearly impossible. On top of that, half their advertisers had begged off—despite Cal's excellent sales pitch about spotlighting the new magazine—so they were going to come in short of revenues *and* pages.

"That's the best you can do?" Cal asked, then listened to what was obviously a negative answer. Every muscle in his body seemed to tense. "I'll get back to you." He hung up without signing off.

"Are we going to press?" Kit asked.

He sighed and leaned back against the high-backed executive chair. For a long time he didn't answer.

In fact, judging from his faraway expression, Kit began to wonder if he'd forgotten she was there at all.

She was about to say something lame, just to jolt him out of his thoughts, when he looked her dead in the eye and said, "There's something you should know."

Oh-oh. She braced herself mentally as much as she could. "What is it?"

"Monahan wants this magazine to fail."

"What?" She couldn't have been more surprised if he'd told her that her hair was on fire. "What do you mean he wants it to fail? Why would he want that?"

Cal gave a half shrug. "It'll be one more tax write-off for him. He would have liquidated the damn thing already if it weren't for the fact that he wanted to humiliate me."

"I'm not following," Kit said, though deep down she was afraid maybe she was.

"Monahan's got…a *little problem* with me," Cal said, confirming Kit's suspicion. "It's personal."

"So personal that he didn't want to raise curiosity by taking you off *Sports World* and canning you entirely, so he put you here hoping you'd fail." The idea burned her up. "Am I close?"

He nodded. "Pretty close."

"Where am I off?"

Cal smiled. How could he look so amused at a time like this? "He wasn't *hoping* I'd fail, he was *sure* I'd fail."

"*This* is *exactly* what's wrong with business in America today," Kit said angrily. "Big corporations run by big fat cats prowl through industry and just *consume* businesses like—" she was running out of ways to keep the analogy going "—like field mice."

Cal looked at her and gave a small laugh. "Sing it, sister."

"Okay, so the analogy was weak. I think better on paper. But you get what I'm saying, don't you?"

"I think so. But you're going to tell me anyway, aren't you?"

Damn right she was. "Monahan didn't give a damn about the people who worked here, the people who had been loyal to *Home Life* for years and even decades. He didn't care who might need their jobs because they lived on a pension or had children to support. He just toyed with *all* of us in order to screw you over. Is that right?"

Cal nodded. "That's one way of putting it."

"He was willing to sacrifice scores of people just because of *one guy.*"

"Look, guys like Monahan have power that extends further than you can imagine. For them it's nothing to reach out and knock someone over, and if other people fall in the process, well…" He shrugged. "That's just the way it goes. Besides, without wanting to humiliate me, he might have just axed the magazine altogether. He only wanted the other companies in the buy anyway."

"That's despicable."

"Maybe. But it's life. And in particular, it's Breck Monahan's life."

She was absolutely aghast. "Has he done this to other people? Other companies?"

"Companies, sure. People—that I don't know."

"So it could be just you."

He nodded.

"My God."

"I know."

She shook her head, hating that she worked in a world where that could happen. Then she raised her gaze again and leveled it right on Cal. "Then we have to beat him at his own game."

Chapter Thirteen

Cal couldn't believe his ears. "You want to take Breck Monahan on?"

Her green eyes focused on him. "Hey, I took you on. It can't be worse than that."

He gave a soft laugh and shook his head. This woman was something else. All his life he'd been surrounded by women who needed to be taken care of. Who took but didn't give.

But now, without even knowing all of the details, Kit Macy was ready to stand by his side and fight Goliath.

Sure, it was a little naive, but he was touched nonetheless.

"You don't want to take him on, much as I appreciate the offer."

She sighed, as if preparing to explain something simple to a very young—or very stupid—child. "Look, Cal, Monahan didn't just affect you with his actions. He affected a lot of people. Not least of which is me. And my son. I'm not going to let him get away with that. Because if he does, I'm going to have to get a job at a fast-food restaurant anyway." She smiled. "So what do I have to lose?"

He had never in his life felt so attracted to a woman.

"So we need to figure out how we're going to accelerate our success enough to save both our jobs," she went on.

"Okay," Cal said, nodding slowly. He'd go ahead and accept this at face value, just this once. "Here's what I'm thinking. Is there anything filed away here that we might be able to tweak a little bit and use?"

"Like Lila Harper's daring exposé of the sweater-vest?" She smiled and shook her head. "I don't think so."

"I'm talking about as a springboard to a new article. *Home Life* published so many patently wrong articles that I'm thinking we could use them to show the danger of misinformation." Cal tapped his fingers against the desk. "For example, what about doing something on the dangers of elderly doctors practicing medicine without keeping up with modern science?"

Kit knew immediately that he was referring to Orville's work. "So you *did* read some of our back issues," Kit said.

"Worse that that. I read the original submissions. Lucky for you guys, someone was here to edit the old guy." He looked at her pointedly.

She warmed under his gaze. "It's not a bad topic. There's certainly a lot to be said on the subject. And I'm sure *Home Life* wasn't the only magazine telling people that aspirin and cola make the young people high." She nodded. "I'll work on it."

"No."

She stopped.

"We need to finish staffing the office. I don't want you handling so much by yourself." He snapped his pen open and started scrawling on the pad on his desk. "Today's Wednesday. I think the deadline for calling ads into the classified section is four o'clock, so that gives us—" he looked at the clock on the wall behind Kit "—an hour. I want you to advertise for two editors, one administrative assistant, maybe three to five more staff writers—use your judgment on that—and a stable of freelancers."

"All by next week?"

"Is that a problem?"

"No." Kit took her PDA out of her purse and started making notes herself. "What kind of writers?"

Concentration etched deeply into Cal's features. "Let's see…we've got you doing your modern-mom thing and I've got Hayward Burns to do a piece on shock jocks—"

"He'd know." Hayward Burns was the worst of them all.

Cal nodded. "Precisely what makes it interesting. We've also got technology and travel covered and I've gotten a handful of useable articles on various things from my old contacts."

"You have?"

He nodded.

"Why haven't I seen them?"

"I'll e-mail them to you. But don't worry—these are pros. They won't require a lot of work on your part."

She'd heard *that* before.

Cal continued. "That leaves us needing a book critic, movie critic, I'd like a cultural columnist covering pop culture—think Dominick Dunne—and a financial advisor. Wait—" he snapped his fingers "—not an ordinary save-for-your-retirement financial advisor, though. I want someone edgy. Don't tell us it's risky to be a day trader, tell us how to do it." He nodded to himself. "I like that."

For the next half hour they discussed Cal's vision for the magazine and who he wanted to hire. He showed her the articles he'd already procured and they discussed the possibilities for placing them and promoting them. Although Kit wasn't one hundred percent on board with all of his suggestions, for the most part she had to agree that his ideas were interesting.

She'd buy the magazine he was proposing if she just saw it on the rack. So that had to be a good sign.

She went back to her office and saw the blinking red light on her phone indicating that a message was waiting.

Her heart leaped to her throat. Her first thought was of Johnny. Although she was lucky enough to have experienced no tragedies with her son, she watched enough news to know that danger was everywhere and she could never be sure he was safe unless he was right in front of her. Normally she kept herself in check and didn't panic until it was absolutely necessary, but for some reason today she had a feeling something bad had happened.

Nervously she lifted the phone and dialed for the messages. It wasn't from the school. For a moment—just a moment—Kit's shoulders sagged in relief.

Then she realized it was from the mortgage company, and the loan officer was saying they had to extend settlement by a month. He didn't think he'd need more paperwork, but he told her to make copies of her latest bank statement just in case.

Which was really unfortunate since she'd had a whole lot of trouble keeping her balance up this month. She'd had to pay the many doctors' bills, utility bills, department store bills for new clothes for Johnny, etc., that she *hadn't* during the previous three months when she'd needed her bank balance to look high and steady.

If she had to give them another month's bank statement, things were going to get ugly. At least for her they were.

She hung up the phone with a new settlement date of August 21, which she figured was at least better than them canceling it altogether, though she still wasn't happy about it.

For now, she just had to concentrate on keeping her job. Cal had given her two months. In a worst-case scenario, that would still be enough time to secure the mortgage.

When she left work at nearly six o'clock that night, she noticed Cal was still in his office. His door was slightly open, and she stopped in the hall and looked at him for a moment.

He was bent over some work on his desk, his face tight with concentration. Or maybe it was concern. From what he'd told her, he had every reason to be concerned. If he failed at making this magazine work, he wouldn't work in the industry again. Or at least not in this town.

And that wasn't fair. Because he was a good worker. If Monahan was worth his salt, he'd count himself lucky to have Cal working for him.

She watched him work for a moment, thinking that as powerful as he was, there was a vulnerability in him, especially right now, that made her want to just go in and put her arms around him.

But that wasn't the sort of relationship they had. As nice as their rapport was at times, Cal kept her at arm's length, and she was going to do the same.

"Can I use the computer now, Mommy?"

Johnny had fulfilled every request Kit had made in an effort to stall for time while she looked Breck Monahan and Cal Panagos up on a search engine. Now he stood there in clean pajamas, his hair and teeth brushed, his hands washed, his room clean, his clothes for tomorrow laid out and his bedtime storybook chosen and prepared.

He'd done everything she'd asked and more.

This was the problem with sharing one computer, even if one of the people sharing only wanted to go on morningTV.com and play Sam Goes to School. "Here's the deal, buddy," Kit said. "I need five more minutes, okay? Then you can have twenty minutes instead of fifteen. That's a whole *twenty.* What do you think?"

"Sure!" With a huge smile he went running off to do some task she had somehow neglected to suggest.

Kit turned back to the Internet and read through the list of articles mentioning both Monahan and Panagos. She was trying to figure out what had happened between the two men so she could hopefully figure out if there was a way to fix it.

Finally she found one article that appeared to be of some relevance in theparlor.com. She printed it out, along with three of the editorial letters Cal had written for *Sports World,* then called Johnny and let him have his time playing educational computer games.

At least she *hoped* they were educational, since she'd been promising him for two hours that if he only waited a few more minutes he could use the computer.

She went to the living room and sat down on the

old easy chair she'd had since college and leaned back to read the articles.

She began with the editorial letters and, though she was impressed with his writing and his clarity of thought, there was nothing there that gave her any clue to what kind of person he was or what he'd done to irk his employer.

The third article, from theparlor.com, was written three months ago by Carrie Singer, a woman who'd evidently met Cal at a publishing party. Unfortunately Carrie Singer had found nothing to fault Cal with, apart from a combination of "lethal good looks" and "razor-sharp wit." It was nothing Kit hadn't already realized, though she couldn't imagine herself going so far as to put it in print.

Carrie Singer was probably a girlfriend of Cal's. Kit made a mental note to bring the name up in front of him and see what his reaction might be. Not that it helped her figure out what had happened with Monahan to put her job in danger.

She couldn't quite explain why she was so interested in finding out tidbits about Cal if they *didn't* relate to her job.

At ten o'clock she gave up for the night and realized that Johnny should have been in bed two hours ago. That was more important than digging up dirt on Breck Monahan where there was none.

Not that she didn't think there was dirt on him *somewhere*. But clearly it wasn't where she was looking tonight.

Then suddenly an idea struck her.

How, in all of their hand-wringing, had she and Cal not already thought of this? It was the only possible solution to their time crunch. Yet it had taken this Cal-worshipping article by Carrie Singer to make Kit see what had to be done.

She had to call Cal. She couldn't wait until tomorrow; she had to get a hold of him quickly so they could start planning right away.

But first, there was Johnny.

She allowed him to play his educational video game for twenty minutes while she formulated her plan on paper so she could present it to Cal coherently.

After that, she led Johnny into his bedroom and gestured toward the bed. "Short story tonight," she said, trying not to let her eagerness to get back to her own work show too much. "You've been up *way* past your bedtime."

"But you didn't tell me to go to bed!"

"I know." She ruffled his hair. "But didn't you get tired?"

"I did...." he admitted.

"Then you should have gone to bed yourself. Just because I said you could play on the computer didn't mean you *had* to. Especially not if you were too tired."

"But I'm not tired anymore."

That was the way it always went. If she didn't catch him during one tiny window of yawning, she might spend whole hours trying to get him to sleep.

"As soon as I turn the lights out, you'll fall right asleep," she said, hoping against hope that this time it would be true.

Johnny gave her a skeptical glance, then tapped on the book she was holding. "Read first."

She smiled privately, knowing she shouldn't let him give commands but at the same time being so pleased that he wanted her to read to him that she couldn't reprimand him for it. *"The Cleaning Bandit,"* she read. "Once there was a boy who wouldn't clean up his toys…"

Cal was just walking into his apartment at nearly eleven o'clock when the telephone rang.

Monahan, he thought bitterly. He probably shouldn't answer it. Then again, if he didn't, he might find out whatever Monahan had to say in some other, more awkward way. Like perhaps on the front page of the *City Post* or something.

He wouldn't put anything past Breck Monahan, at least while the man had the upper hand.

But it wasn't Breck.

"Cal?" a voice he recognized immediately said. "This is Kit Macy. I'm sorry to call you so late but I didn't think it could wait."

Unless she somehow knew the building where *Real Life* was headquartered was on fire, he couldn't imagine what she might have to say that couldn't wait, so he was immediately on edge. "What's wrong?" he asked her.

"Nothing's wrong," she said quickly. "Actually I think I'm calling with good news."

He'd have to reserve judgment on that.

Come to think of it, maybe it would be good news if the building *was* on fire.

"I have an idea for building our readership faster," Kit went on, her voice tinged with excitement. "We take it online."

"Online?"

"Yes, you know, like theparlor.com and every other print magazine in the United States except for *Home Life.*"

He pinched the bridge of his nose to try and stave off the headache he felt coming on. "I always assumed we'd go online eventually, if we have enough success to stay afloat. How is this any different from any other online magazine?"

"The difference is, we premiere it online and we

keep it online only. At least at first. That way we save a ton of overhead, we don't have to worry about the printer's delay on the first issue and we can designate some of that money to hire someone to do an advertising blitz."

Cal's grasp on the telephone tightened. He walked across the room and stopped at the window. "You might be onto something."

"I'm sure of it. Look, with the extra time we can buy ourselves by putting the first issue online and generating interest, we can make sure we have a really high-quality product." She sounded confident. He could almost picture the glow in her eyes and the flush in her cheeks. "If we rush the first issue to print and it looks lousy, we've blown it. You only have one chance to make a first impression."

He laughed at the earnestness with which she delivered the cliché. "This might work," he conceded slowly, imagining the possibilities.

"Honestly, Cal, I think it's our only chance."

He wasn't quite sharing her enthusiasm, but he was starting to feel the merit of the idea. There were still hurdles, though. Important ones. "We need a Web designer."

"Done. I know one who has a lot of experience with this kind of thing and I think we can get him for a good rate."

This sounded too easy. "I don't want it to be amateurish," he said, hoping for solid reassurance. "Any idiot can put up a Web site. I don't want it to look like a high school newsletter."

"It won't," Kit said quickly. "No way."

"Then get your people together and bring them in tomorrow. Let's set this plan in motion."

"Yes!"

Cal was struck by her enthusiasm. "Kit?"

"Hmm?"

He turned away from the window and sat down on the leather sofa he'd paid about a thousand bucks too much for last year. "I know why *I* want to make this work, but I'm curious—what is it that's making you so invested?"

She hesitated for a fraction of a second. "I told you before, I need my job."

"Yeah, I remember you said that, but this job is ending up being far from ideal and it really doesn't pay that much, so why are you sticking around?"

She hesitated again, and Cal got the distinct impression that she didn't want to tip her hand and reveal any sort of vulnerability.

But then she spoke frankly. "Remember that statement I needed from you that day you agreed to keep me on? The letter stating I'm gainfully employed?"

He remembered; it was one of the first things they'd talked about. Privately he'd really gotten a kick out of her having the nerve to make such a request when he was barely giving her a job. "I remember," he said, smiling to himself.

"Well, I needed that for a mortgage I've applied for."

"But you got it. So theoretically it doesn't matter what happens to your job now, at least as far as the bank is concerned. They have the letter and that answers that."

"Normally," she agreed. "But nothing about this has been normal. Settlement is supposed to be at the end of this month, but one loan officer left, and the new one isn't all that receptive. And now they're asking for more and more documentation. It's just…anyway, it's a long boring story. The upshot is that if I lose my job, I lose my house. I'll do absolutely anything I can to prevent that from happening."

Cal closed his eyes.

She was going to lose her house.

The woman was a single mother and—from everything he could tell—a really good person, and she was counting on *him* and, more to the point, the success of this dud of a magazine to save her home.

It was almost impossible to imagine a happy ending to this.

"Hello?" she said, interrupting his thoughts. "Cal? Are you still there?"

"I'm here," he said, wishing he was anywhere else. "But, uh, look…it's late and I've got to go. I'll see you tomorrow at the office, okay?"

Chapter Fourteen

Kit spent almost the entire weekend sitting next to the pool—cell phone in one hand, PDA in the other—while Johnny played in the water. The meeting with Cal, Joanna and Parker about starting up a Web site had gone very well, with Parker presenting a bunch of ideas that hadn't even occurred to Cal and Kit. It was immediately clear that Parker had an artistic sensibility along with good, solid practicality. By the end of the conversation, even Jo had agreed to come on board to help with design until her classes began in September.

Which left Kit to try and organize their needs before interviewing staff in two days, all the while watching Johnny wave for her attention and say over and over again, "Look, Mom!" before jumping into the pool, perilously close to the wall.

It was more nerve-racking than the office problems.

After watching Johnny's twentieth cannonball into the pool on Sunday, Kit turned to her PDA and the e-mails that had come in response to her newspaper ad. Probably a good seventy percent of the responses were so illiterate that she wasn't even going to bother with anything more than an automated response.

Three of the response e-mails were obscene. Which Kit found interesting, in a detached sort of way. Not one, not two, but *three* different people had trolled the Help Wanted ads, zeroed in on her editorial request and had decided she was the ideal recipient for suggestions of lewd sexual acts.

Two of them had given phone numbers.

It was amazing. And if it weren't for the handful of good, solid candidates she'd tagged, she would have been really discouraged.

"Hey, Mom." Johnny ran up to Kit, shaking water drops across her. "Can I get a soda?"

"I brought juice," Kit said. "It's healthier. Why don't you sit down and have some along with your cheese sandwich and apples, okay?"

"Can I get ice cream then?" Everything was a negotiation with him.

"No." She sat up and took out the small cooler she'd packed his lunch in. "The apple is dessert."

"Uh-*uh!*" He followed her reluctantly to the picnic tables, where his friend Pete was sitting eating a considerably more exciting-looking lunch that included chips and a sweet packaged dessert.

Pete's mother greeted Kit and they chatted for a moment while Kit set Johnny's lunch out.

She was interrupted by Johnny pulling on her beach cover-up. "Mom, look, that guy's here."

"What guy?" She popped a slice of apple into her mouth.

"*That* guy." He pointed.

She looked and was astonished to see Cal Panagos coming toward her. For a moment she thought it must just be a weird coincidence and that he was there for some other reason, but when he spotted her, he waved.

He was so out of place that she almost didn't recognize him at first. What on earth was Cal Panagos doing at her community pool on a Sunday afternoon?

She quickly asked Pete's mother to keep an eye on Johnny, to which she got ready agreement and the slightest lift of the eyebrow which said Pete's mother wanted some details on this guy later.

The rumor mills were going to start churning in Mom Central.

"What are you *doing* here?" Kit asked, approaching Cal from behind the chain-link fence. She realized immediately that she'd probably sounded rude, so she changed her tone and tried again. "What are you *doing* here?" Forget it. She just couldn't hide her shock.

He laughed. "Surprised to see me?"

"Yes, if you're looking for me."

He gave her a look that clearly said, *Who else would I be looking for?* "I stopped by your apartment and a little old man with a bunch of screwdrivers in his belt loops told me I'd probably find you here."

Mr. Finnegan, no doubt. He didn't want to spring for a tool belt, so when he was working around the place he stuck his tools in his pockets and belt loops. She and Johnny had passed him on the way out. "This seems like a long way out of your way," she said. "Why didn't you just call?"

"I tried. It didn't even ring, it kept going straight to your voice mail service." He shrugged. "I must have left at least three or four messages. Look, I need to talk to you. You want to come out here or should I go in there?" He raked his gaze over her, lingering for a fraction of a second on her legs. Just long enough for her to get gooseflesh and feel embarrassed.

"My apartment is right there," she said, realizing immediately that he knew where her apartment was since he'd just come from there. "Let me just make sure someone can watch Johnny." She hurried back to Johnny, secured supervision for him, then stopped to pick up her things. Her cell phone was there, sitting in a small pool of water where Johnny had come and stood by her at one point, dripping.

Five minutes later Cal was following Kit into her small, hot apartment.

"I'm really sorry to stop by like this but we've got a huge opportunity tonight and we can't let it slip away."

No sooner were the words *slip away* out of his mouth before Kit stepped on something sharp, turned her ankle and lost her balance, falling right back into Cal's arms.

She stumbled backward and clapped her hands in an unfortunate place for Cal. In turn, he doubled over, scooping her into his arms and grazing her breasts with his hands.

The fall seemed to take forever, moving one frame at a time until finally they landed in a heap in the entry hall.

The heavy steel front door banged shut behind them.

Kit scrambled to an upright position. "Oh, my gosh, I'm so sorry. Are you okay?"

"Fine." He winced. "Just give me a minute." He blew a quick breath out. "What the hell happened?"

Only then did she realize that there was a sharp pain in the toes of her right foot. She examined it and pulled out a tiny plastic cannon. She recognized it right away as a piece from a toy Johnny had gotten from a fast-food restaurant. "So much for these being safe for kids three and over. They should come with a warning for adults."

"What is it?" Cal took the item from her and looked at it closely, then burst into laughter. "A *cannon?*"

She nodded. "It's Pelinore Pirate week at Mac-Quickies Fast Food."

"Pelinore?"

"I think it was too expensive to get licensing to use a pirate anyone had heard of."

He laughed again and stood up, slapping the dust off his pants. "You're okay now?" He reached down for her hand and helped her up. "No tiny cannon balls lodged between your toes?"

Now it was her turn to laugh. "There could be— who knows?"

He looked at the toy again. "This is really hard, sharp plastic."

"All the cheaper to make it with." She looked up into his eyes. "I really am sorry if I hurt you. There was no time to react or break my fall." She noticed then that her bathing suit top was twisted and she hastened to fix it, losing her footing slightly in the process.

He reached for her shoulders and steadied her. "Good thing I was there to do it for you."

She nodded. "You saved my butt. Twice now."

He gave a sly smile. "If you see the good china falling, you try and catch it so it doesn't break."

So he was comparing her behind to good china. And she was actually flattered.

She wasn't sure which was worse.

"Thanks." She looked up into his eyes. They were a clearer, softer blue up close than she'd realized. Like brushed denim. "I think."

His mouth curved slowly and his gaze swept over her features, landing on her lips for a moment before he looked into her eyes. "You're welcome. Anytime. Care to take a tumble again?"

She raised an eyebrow. "I'm not falling for you."

He cocked his head. "You've done it before."

She suppressed a smile. "And I nearly got hurt."

"That's the chance you take." He rubbed his thumbs gently against the skin of her upper arm. "Sometimes it's worth it."

"Maybe when you're eighteen. When you're

older and have more responsibility, you have to be really careful not to break *anything*. Can't afford to be laid up."

"There's a lot to be said for being laid down, though." His gaze felt like a caress.

God help her, she wanted him to kiss her.

For a long moment they stood looking at each other, neither advancing nor retreating, his hands still warm against her skin.

Then, when she couldn't resist any longer, Kit reached toward him and in an instant he moved to pull her in in one swift but gentle motion, drawing her against his hard, muscled chest.

She trailed her hands up his back and pulled him closer still, languishing in the sensation of his body against hers, his lips against hers, his breath mingling with hers.

She parted her lips under his mouth and he went with her, touching his tongue to hers lightly at first, tentatively. Then he cupped her face with his hands and deepened the kiss.

He knew just what to do.

And Kit knew she should avoid men who knew just what to do, but still...

He tangled his fingers in her hair, sending tingles straight down her spine as his fingertips tickled against her.

Kit lowered her hands on his back, feeling her way across the supple muscles of his shoulders to the hard plane of his lower back. His skin was warm, even through the thin cotton of his shirt, and she wanted to feel it against her.

She curved against him, knowing she was teasing them both. This couldn't go further. She didn't have room for this in her life. As a working single mother, she barely had room for *herself.* They shouldn't even be doing *this,* but it was so delicious she wanted to enjoy just a few more minutes before the inevitable moment when they agreed this was a crazy impulse that they would never follow again.

But in the meantime…

Finally it was Kit who drew back first, breathless. Her whole body felt flushed and tingling, her muscles relaxed to the point of feeling like noodles, as if she'd spent too much time in a Jacuzzi.

Looking at him, his eyes lit with desire, she was tempted to give right back in to the temptation, but logic stopped her.

"This is crazy."

"It could be crazier."

"It almost was," Kit said, reaching for a towel from the pile she'd put on the foyer table earlier when she and Johnny had been getting ready to leave. She wrapped it around her shoulders, glad for the illusion of modesty.

"Would that really be so bad?" He shrugged. "No, you're right. That was stupid."

She didn't recall actually saying it was *stupid,* but she decided to go with that rather than get into yet another battle with him over semantics. "Then we're agreed."

He gave a single nod. "Absolutely."

"Good." She drew the towel closer around her. "Now what's this opportunity you were talking about?"

His expression shifted instantly to one she recognized as all business. "Max Trilling is going to be in town tonight for a reception over at Warner Hall."

"Max Trilling, the crime writer?"

"And court reporter and opinion columnist and old Hollywood fixture, yes." He ticked Trilling's accomplishments off on his fingers. "I want you to go to this reception, wheedle your way in and use your considerable charms to convince him to give us an exclusive on the upcoming Sissy Searles trial."

Sissy Searles was a former child star who had recently been accused of murdering a B-list actor she'd claimed to have a relationship with. The case was rumored to have more bizarre twists and turns than the *Twilight Zone* episode in which she'd made her debut.

"Why can't you do it?"

"Monahan's going to be there. If he sees me talking to Trilling and figures out what I'm doing, he'll sabotage the whole thing."

"What did you *do* to him?"

Cal shook his head. "Let's just stick to the subject at hand, okay? The reception starts in two hours. That's just enough time for you to shower up and do whatever it is you women do to get ready and get into town."

Two hours! "I can't do that," Kit said, though she did agree he had a point that it would be great to get Trilling's coverage of the trial. "I've got Johnny."

"Johnny?" Cal's expression was blank.

"Yes, my son. I can't find a sitter at the last minute on a Sunday night. Not one I know and trust anyway." She didn't add that she went out so seldom that she didn't really know *any* sitters.

"I'll take him," Cal said quickly.

Kit couldn't help it, she laughed. "Oh? Do you have any experience with kids? Apart from the occasional eavesdropping you do on Parents Alone meetings, I mean."

He gave her a look, then said, "No, I don't have a lot of experience, but how hard can it be? The kid's—what—five? Six?"

"Four."

"Piece of cake. I'll take him for ice cream while you're at the reception."

"I don't know...."

"Kit, come on. You need this magazine to succeed as much as I do. You *know* this is a great opportunity. We can't just let this chance slip away. And frankly, Kit, you're the only one who can do this."

It was true. "Okay, here's the deal," she said. "If you take Johnny, you watch him every second—do you understand? Don't let him out of your sight for a moment, not even in the bathroom. The city is a dangerous place and it only takes nine seconds for someone to snatch a kid and disappear forever."

Cal made the motion of crossing his heart. "I won't let him out of my sight for a second. I won't even blink."

"I'm *serious* about this."

"Me, too. Don't worry about it, I'll take care of him. How hard could it be?"

She wasn't that worried about how hard it would be for him, as long as he kept her baby safe. "Let's go out and introduce you to Johnny. If he's comfortable with this arrangement then we'll do it."

"Don't worry about it," Cal said with absolute— and, Kit suspected, potentially misguided—confidence. "Johnny and I will have a great time."

Chapter Fifteen

It should have occurred to Cal that the line at Serendipity would have been so long *before* he'd gotten Johnny Macy all excited about the frozen hot chocolate.

"Think you'd like to go somewhere else and get a sundae?" he asked the child.

"No, thanks," Johnny replied, looking at the array of tacky gifts on the shelves of the waiting area. "What's this?" He picked up a glass figurine of what looked like a cross between a ballerina and a goat.

"Whoa, buddy." Cal took the glass from the boy and set it carefully back on the shelf. "Gotta be careful."

Johnny shrugged and immediately began fingering another glass item. Then another. Each time, Cal had to swoop in and try and save it until finally it was Cal himself who—in an effort to stop one from falling—knocked five of the figurines to the floor.

He suspected it was because the host wanted to preserve the merchandise that Johnny and Cal were given a table about three minutes later.

Cal sat down and took out his phone to see if there were any missed calls.

"Why do you keep looking at your phone?" Johnny asked.

"Just looking to see if your mom called."

"Wouldn't you hear it?"

He'd been asking himself the same thing all night. It felt like hours since they'd dropped Kit off at the reception, but in fact it had only been one hour. She might not call for another hour or even two. Hell, if she hit it off with Max Trilling, Cal could end up babysitting late into the evening.

"Huh? Wouldn't you?"

Cal turned his attention back to the boy. "Wouldn't I what?"

"Hear the phone ringing?"

Cal nodded. "Probably." He set the phone down on the table. "I'll just leave it here to make sure."

Johnny shrugged and a big smile came over his

face as the waiter approached the table and asked what they wanted.

Fifteen minutes later there was a frozen hot chocolate and a black coffee on the table, and the waiter had explained that since it was the dinner hour, there was a minimum table order. Fortunately the five figurines Cal had smashed—and which had been swept into a bag and presented to him—more than covered the difference.

"So…" Cal searched for something to say to the boy, who was eagerly shoveling spoonfuls of frozen chocolate into his mouth and onto his face and clothes. "Are you in school?"

"Kinda." Another huge mouthful went in.

Cal got an ice-cream headache just watching it.

"What do you mean *kinda?*"

"I *do* go to a school, but it's not a very good one and my mom says I get to go to a new one when we get our new house and that's gonna be a lot better because there won't be a Ms. Phillips there *or* a Kyle Cherkins."

Cal figured Ms. Phillips was a teacher or something. "Who's Kyle Cherkins?"

"A boy. He's a hideous little bully."

Cal nearly laughed aloud to hear what were surely Kit's own words coming out of her boy's mouth, but it was clear that this was no laughing matter to Johnny. "He's in your class?"

"He's *everywhere.*" Johnny reached his spoon into his bowl and got a wobbly bit of whipped cream on it. "I wish I had superpowers so I could make him stop."

Suddenly Cal's amusement disappeared. He was touched by the boy's serious countenance as he spoke, even though it was smeared with chocolate and whipped cream. "What superpowers would you have if you could pick?"

Johnny didn't even have to pause to think about it. "I'd be invisible. Then I could trip Kyle, and Ms. Phillips wouldn't see me and blame me for everything instead of him."

Cal was a little amazed at how readily he climbed onto the anti–Ms. Phillips and anti–Kyle Cherkins trains. "What about super speed, so you could do it really fast and then run back to the other side of the room before the teacher caught you?"

Johnny's eyes grew wide. *"Yeah!"*

"That way you could also win all the races on Olympic Day."

"What's Olymmicday?"

"I guess that comes a little later. In elementary school. That's the day when all the kids run races and obstacle courses and stuff. My grades weren't so good when I was a kid, but I used to be *great* on Olympic Day."

"I'll be good at it, too," Johnny said confidently. "*Especially* if I get my super-speed powers."

Cal looked dubiously at the nearly gone frozen hot chocolate—the menu suggested it would serve two—and said, "If you want to be like a superhero, you're probably better off having spinach and stuff instead of ice cream."

"That's what my mom says *all the time*," Johnny said, with a nod of acknowledgment.

"Yeah?" Cal smiled thinking about Kit and Johnny interacting. "What else does your mom say?"

"That I shouldn't lead the dog to my room by his tail."

Cal smiled. "That's true. What else?"

Johnny crinkled his nose as he thought about it. "That she can't stand the guy on TV."

"Which guy?"

"You know. The one that always says, *Who's gotcha covered?*"

The imitation of TV talking head and political commentator William Ryan was so good that Cal gave a shout of laughter. "She's right about him, too." And how. Will Ryan was one of Breck Mona-han's best buddies and together they seemed to think they ruled the entire world of media. "She doesn't like him, huh? Tell me more."

"I don't know." Johnny belched and his hand flew to his mouth. "'Scuse me," he said guiltily.

"Johnny, you never need to excuse yourself when you do that in front of a guy."

"I *don't?*"

Cal got a quick vision of the reaming Kit would give him if she knew he was telling her son things like that. "Not in front of me, anyway. You like your ice cream? Want some more?"

"I'm full."

"Next time then."

Johnny smiled wide. He had bits of chocolate stuck between his little teeth. "We can do this *again?*"

"Sure," Cal said and realized he meant it. "This was fun." He signaled the waiter for the check.

"I thought of something else about my mom," Johnny volunteered a few minutes later while Cal signed the exorbitant check.

"What's that?"

"She works near my school."

"Hey, that means I do, too."

Johnny frowned. "You *do?*"

"Sure." Cal pocketed his wallet and stood up. "I work with your mom."

"'Kay. So is her boss your boss? She loves her boss."

Everything stopped for a moment. Was the child being sarcastic? "She what?"

"She loves her boss," Johnny said, standing up beside Cal. He was really covered in chocolate stains. Kit shouldn't have sent him out for ice cream in that white T-shirt.

"How do you know that?"

"Because she *told* me," Johnny said as if it was the most ridiculous question ever. "She *always* talks about how great he is and how much she loves him."

It was embarrassing how much this pleased Cal. He knew there were sparks flying between himself and Kit, he'd just figured they were the kind you got when you struck flint to flint really hard. He'd never dreamed she actually had positive—in fact, *very* positive—feelings about him.

Although that kiss had certainly been hot.

Come to think of it, people didn't share that kind of passion purely out of combustion together. There *had* to be some romantic energy behind it or it just wouldn't happen.

At least, it wouldn't have felt the way it did.

"That's nice," Cal said. "But maybe you shouldn't tell her you said anything to me about that."

"Why not?"

Cal gave half a shrug. "You don't want to embarrass her by telling her people know her secret."

"It's not a *secret*," Johnny said, instinctively reaching for Cal's hand as they walked out of the restaurant.

The feel of his little warm hand in Cal's was unexpectedly pleasant. He'd never thought of kids as being fun to have around, but he had to admit this one was pretty cute.

"She tells everyone."

Cal imagined Johnny overhearing Kit talking to her girlfriends. "But maybe she wouldn't want you to tell me."

"She doesn't care. Everyone knows she loves Mr. Markham. *I* love him, too. He always gives me those red-and-white peppermints to eat."

Cal groaned inwardly. Ebbit Markham. Of course. Johnny thought old Ebbit was still his mom's boss.

Cal's phone rang, startling him with its chirpy ring. He'd never noticed how much it sounded like a tiny little laugh. "Panagos," he said, trying to make up for his embarrassment by using his best gruff-executive voice.

"Score!" Kit whispered excitedly into the phone. "We've got him. Now come pick me up quick before he finds me. If he has one more drink, I'm afraid he's going to try and do a tonsil probe on me with his tongue."

"We're on the way," Cal said, clapping the phone closed. "Come on, kid. Your mama's waiting."

"It's really simple. All you have to do is dip the corner of a napkin into the water they put on your table anyway and wipe his face and clothes off with it. It's not exactly brain surgery." Kit was coming into her living room with two cups of coffee. She set one down on the coffee table in front of Cal.

Johnny had fallen into a post-sugar coma shortly after they'd gotten back to Kit's apartment.

"I'm not a parent. I don't know these things."

She laughed. "It's common sense. It's not like I got a manual when he was born telling me how to clean him."

"All right, all right. Tell me about Trilling."

She took a sip of her coffee and set the mug down. "Turns out he was on the outs with Polowski over at *Another View*. He wants to stick it to Polowski by getting on board with an upstart with a huge marketing campaign. We *do* have a huge marketing campaign coming, don't we? Have you talked to that ad agency?"

"It's all in place," Cal confirmed. "Huge blitz— billboards, print ads, the whole nine yards."

"Good, because that's what I said." Kit smiled at him. "Do you know we might actually be able to pull this off."

"Of course we will," Cal said with a confidence he barely felt. But he *was* beginning to feel the rumblings of optimism, and it had been a very long time since he'd felt anything like that.

She eyed him keenly. "You don't sound as if you're sure you mean that."

"Give me time. I really want to believe it."

She shrugged. "Sometimes that's the best you can hope for."

He looked into her eyes and thought to himself that she deserved a whole lot more than just to hope to believe. Kit Macy was a really special woman. He kept learning it in different ways, at different times. His time tonight with Johnny had shown him a whole other side to Kit. It was almost like a puzzle piece he hadn't quite been able to envision before meeting her son and seeing her expressions and reactions played out on the smaller canvas.

"So it sounds like you and Johnny had a good time tonight," Kit said, as if reading his mind.

"He's a great kid," Cal said. "Reminds me a lot of his mother."

She raised her eyebrows. "But you still think he's a great kid, huh?"

Cal smiled. "Apart from that small hurdle, yeah."

She looked into his eyes and he felt something stir within him. Again. He wanted to kiss her.

And yet, really the last thing in the world he wanted to do was kiss her. He didn't even want to *want* to kiss her. That could *only* complicate things—he'd learned that lesson all too well. In fact, he'd learned it *without* having this intense compulsion toward the woman, so this could only bring about his ruin.

He'd have to be a fool to take that chance. To squander his own last chance at success on this fleeting physical desire for a woman.

No matter how attractive she was. No matter how smart. No matter how funny or how strong or how admirable in a hundred other ways.

"Cal? Is everything okay?"

"Y-yes. Yeah, it's fine, I was just thinking about something. I've got to go." He started to stand.

"But—" Kit scrambled to her feet, clearly puzzled. "I thought we were going to devise our plans for Trilling."

"We'll do that." Cal nodded. "There's time. It's just—I've been away a long time today, what with the whole pool, ice cream, reception, coffee thing, and I've just remembered I have some things I need to do to prepare for our interviews tomorrow."

"Oh. Okay." Kit followed him to the door. "I'll see you in the morning then."

"See if you can get in a little early, would you?" Cal thought it was important to maintain the boss demeanor that seemed to annoy her so much. Not like Ebbit Markham, who'd probably handed out lollipops at staff meetings. "We've got a lot to do."

Her expression dimmed slightly. "I'll be there."

"Good." Cal gave a nod and left, walking into the balmy night. He didn't know why he did it, but when he got to the sidewalk and was almost to his car, he stopped and looked back.

There in the window, framed by the venetian blinds he was holding open with his small hands, was Johnny, smiling and trying to wave without letting the blinds close.

Cal smiled and waved back, but inside his heart gave an uncomfortable flip.

He knew it wasn't possible that Monahan had anticipated what would happen, but the truth of the matter remained. If Monahan had wanted to trap Cal on the very grounds he was using to oust him—specifically his weakness for a woman—he couldn't have picked better bait, it turned out, than Kit Macy.

But it wasn't about her looks—it was her wit; the way she challenged him; the fact that, around her, he was forced to do his best, to *be* his best. She made him feel better about himself.

Kit Macy—and even her son—brought out the best in Cal.

And that scared him to death.

Chapter Sixteen

The interviews were a lot more work than Kit had expected.

She'd interviewed job applicants before, of course. Hired an administrative assistant here, a staff writer there. Certainly she'd had her hand in acquiring a lot of freelance articles. But sitting in her office interviewing one person after another in rapid succession was exhausting. By the end of the day, though she'd found several excellent prospects, she'd also called three different interviewees by the wrong name. It was a mistake she seldom made, much less three different times with three different people in one day.

After her last interview, she went to Cal's office,

where he was sitting behind his desk tossing a squishy stress ball from one hand to the other and looking about as exhausted as she felt.

"Finished?" Kit asked after a quiet knock.

He looked up and waved her in. "And then some." He tossed the stress ball onto his desk, where it landed with a dull thud.

She smiled and plunked down in the chair opposite him. "I think we did well, though. Covered all of our bases." It felt good, this camaraderie. A few weeks ago she wouldn't have believed it was possible, but she genuinely felt as if she and Cal were in this together.

It felt good.

Really good.

He let out a long sigh. "Yeah. I guess we did all right. At this point I'm so burned out I can't even remember who I hired."

"You e-mailed me a list."

He pinched the bridge of his nose and yawned. "I should have copied myself on it."

She laughed gently. "I'll send it back to you." She took a deep breath. It was time for her to leave, but she didn't want to go quite yet. "So…I guess I'm going to hit the road now. Unless you can think of anything else we need to cover first?"

He shook his head. "If anything comes up, I can

handle it. I know you've got to get home to Johnny."
He smiled and shook his head, more to himself than
to her. "Great kid."

Kit was touched at Cal's affection for her son.
"Actually Johnny's staying at his dad's house again
tonight, so I'm on my own."

Cal glanced up at her with a light in his eye that
made Kit's heart skip a beat, but before he could say
anything, his secretary buzzed.

"Mr. Panagos, Mr. Zo is here to see you about
writing a political column."

He glanced at Kit and she shrugged.

"We're not doing a regular political column," he
said.

"I tried to tell him that, sir, but he insists on seeing you."

"Send him in." Cal lifted his hand from the button and looked at Kit. "Care to stick around for Mr.
Zo's interview?"

"Why not? I'd love to see how you handle interviews when you actually *want* to hire rather than
fire."

"Cute, Kit."

"Thanks, Cal."

He shot her a look just as the door opened and a
narrow little bald man, wearing thick black glasses

and a black soul patch of hair right under his bottom lip, walked in.

He possessed a strange air of self-righteousness and Kit felt uncomfortable with him immediately.

"Mr. Panagos, I have some things to say and I think you and your readers need to hear it." He brushed past Kit and stood in front of Cal's desk.

"This is Ms. Macy," Cal said, pointing out Kit. "And if you have something to say to me and my readers, then you have something to say to her, too. You might start with an introduction."

The man gave a quick nod to Kit and handed her a folder. "Here's my résumé, which will introduce me, though it shouldn't really matter. Now, Mr. Panagos, like most Americans, I'm fed up with the current administration and I think it's time we all called the spade by its name."

Mixed metaphors aside, the man reeked of lunacy. Kit exchanged puzzled looks with Cal, then opened the folder. There, at the top of the page it said *Beau Zeau, writer and American political activist.*

Beau Zeau.

It took Kit a moment, then she stifled a laugh and handed it to Cal with a nod toward it. Wordlessly he opened it, glanced at the page inside, then closed it again and looked back at the man who was still talking in front of him.

"Excuse me, Mr...?"

"Zeau."

"Yes, Mr. Zeau. Beau Zeau." Cal shook his head. "Bozo. That's pretty good. Now, what's your game? Why are you here?"

One might have expected the man to crack a smile and explain that he was joking or at least making a point in a humorous way, but instead he stayed very serious. Almost comically serious. "I think it's obvious, Mr. Panagos, I'm out to let the world know about the bozos in charge of our government. It's time to *expose* them and make them pay for what they've done."

Kit felt a little nervous tremor cross her chest at the man's vehemence, but Cal merely sighed.

"Look, I don't know which bozos you're referring to and frankly I don't want to know. *Real Life* isn't a political platform for you or anyone else to spread negativity from. Sorry, but I'm going to have to ask you to leave."

The small man crossed his arms in front of him and stood his ground. "Not until I've been heard and understood."

Cal stood up and walked to him. "You've been heard and I'm pretty sure Ms. Macy and I understand you, as well. Thanks for coming by." He took the man by the arm and led him out the door as easily as if he were a rag doll.

Kit turned to watch him lead the man to the elevator, deposit him onto it and push the buttons inside.

The doors closed as the self-proclaimed Beau Zeau was protesting his oppression, and Cal said to his secretary, "Call security and tell them to watch for that bozo and escort him out. Then you might as well knock off. There's nothing else for you to do today."

Kit felt a surge of new appreciation for Cal. Okay, admiration. He'd certainly handled that smoothly and without any hint of feeling unnerved, the way she was.

It was sexy.

He came back in, shut the door behind him, sat down behind his desk and looked at Kit. "I hope there are no more of those."

She smiled. "Oh, Cal, the world is *full* of those. Mrs. Zeau is probably on her way up right now."

They looked at each other and started laughing at the same time.

Kit was struck by the ease she felt with him, the solidarity. Cal had made her so nervous at first, but the more she worked with him, the more she found she just plain liked him. Even when he was difficult, she got a kick out of him.

"I don't know if this is going to work out, Ms. Macy, but it sure has been interesting."

"Why, Mr. Panagos, you have to think positive thoughts!"

"I may need a little help with that." Cal opened his desk drawer and took out a bottle of good tequila and two shot glasses. He filled both of them and skidded one across the desk to Kit.

She shook her head. "I never drink at work."

He downed his and refilled it. "No?" He leveled a simmering gaze on her. "I bet there are a lot of good things you've never done at work."

Electricity crackled between them.

"For example?" she asked.

"You tell me."

Kit cleared her throat. "I'm *not* going to get into a game of *I Never* with you."

He looked puzzled. "A game of what?"

"*I Never.* You know, when one person says something they've never done and if the other person has they have to drink. And everyone has to tell the truth. *I Never.*" She shrugged. "Don't tell me you've never played."

"Nope."

She couldn't believe it. "Didn't you go to college?"

"Apparently it was before the *I Never* craze swept the nation. We were still limited to playing *Quarters.*"

Kit shook her head. "You missed out." Dubiously

she eyed the shot glass that still sat on the desk in front of her.

"So you'd do what? Say something like—I don't know—I never gave birth?" He looked at her, then at the glass in front of her.

She sighed and after a moment drank from the glass in front of her. "There. You've got it. And if I said, um, I never angered my boss so much that he'd be willing to sink an entire business in order to get back at me, you'd have to—" she nodded toward his glass "—you know."

He drank the shot in front of him, then refilled his own and hers. "Like that?"

She smiled and nodded. "Just like that."

"Wait, I've got another one. I never…" He paused and thought about it.

She looked at him, knowing she should leave before things went any further but unable to resist the impulse to stick around and see what he'd come up with next.

Especially since he was losing and soon he might admit exactly what it was that had happened with Monahan.

"I never…kept a job I didn't want with a boss I couldn't stand just so I could buy a house."

"Touché," she said after having just a long sip instead of the whole shot glass.

Cal didn't call her on it. She supposed it was the difference between college and real life. At least, if one was still going to be playing something as inane as *I Never* in real life.

"I've got another one," Cal said, watching her. "I never changed my mind about not being able to stand my boss."

Kit looked at him steadily for a moment before raising the glass to her lips.

He smiled.

Her stomach flipped.

"My turn," she said, hoping he'd had enough tequila to loosen him up to the point where she might push the envelope a little. "I never had an affair at work."

Cal remained still.

Kit was glad, though she was hard-pressed to explain why.

After a moment he raised his eyebrows and said, "I never…let's see here…I never had a sexual fantasy about my boss."

Kit made a move to pick up her shot glass, then froze. She *had,* in fact, had a sexual fantasy about her boss. Maybe—just maybe—even more than one.

Now she had two choices. She could play this game fairly or she could play it in order to present the self she wanted him to believe existed.

It wasn't a quick and easy decision.

Eventually she decided on honesty. Not because it was the moral thing to do so much as something in the look in his eye made her want to goad him.

She took a sip.

He raised his eyebrows. "Can I have another turn?" he asked, his mouth curling toward a smile.

She shook her head. "It's my turn. I never had a sexual fantasy about one of my employees."

He didn't even hesitate. He reached right for his shot glass and took a drink.

Kit was beginning to feel ever so slightly woozy from telling the truth, so it might have been because of that that she wanted to be more specific.

But he cut her off before she could beat him to the punch.

"I never..." Cal leaned forward slightly toward Kit, and lowered his voice to a husky quiet that sent chills down her spine. "I never had sex in the office."

When she reached for her glass this time, her hand shook slightly. But it wasn't nerves that had her on edge, it was excitement. Or anticipation. Or some measure of both.

"I never tried to seduce my managing editor," she said boldly, looking him in the eye as he lifted his glass.

When he drank she felt a not-too-small measure of triumph.

This was fun.

This was *really* fun.

Cal swiped the back of his hand across his mouth, drizzling a few drops from his glass across the table before setting the glass down hard. "Okay, I never decided to say no to someone I was attracted to just because they were my boss."

Kit held his gaze, and though she reached for her glass, she couldn't bring herself to lift it.

"Can I be more specific?" he asked.

"Not until it's your turn," Kit returned.

He swallowed and took what sounded like a tight breath.

She recognized it because she was feeling the same way.

Kit looked at Cal for a long moment before saying, "I never wanted to be with someone so badly that I was willing to risk huge rejection to let them know."

Cal's hesitation was short, then one corner of his mouth turned up into a wry smile and he lifted his glass to her as if in a toast. "You got me there," he said.

A thrill ran straight through Kit, all the way from her spine to her toes.

"Your turn," she said, though her voice was barely audible.

Cal set his glass down and slowly stood up, walking around his desk deliberately until he stood in front of her.

He leaned against the desk and looked down into Kit's eyes, just a foot or two away in actuality but in some ways feeling as if he was on another planet.

"I never intended to say no to Cal Panagos when he wanted to kiss me," he said softly.

Kit took a long, slow breath. There was no keeping up the pretense now.

She didn't touch her glass.

Cal moved toward her and put his hands on her shoulders to draw her in as he bent down to her. His mouth covered hers with a singularity of purpose she'd never quite felt before.

Kit felt all of the energy she'd poured into opposing him suddenly melt and turn into hot, molten desire for him. There wasn't a part of her body that didn't desire his touch; there wasn't a part of her that didn't need this connection with him.

He tapped a control on the wall behind his desk, turning off the overhead lights. Then he went and knelt before her, drawing her out of her seat and against him. His kiss was slow and sensuous. Kit went with it, the way one would go with a roller-coaster ride—a little nervous and a little excited all at the same time, with a sense of inevitability thrown in to make all of her wrestling with right/wrong and good/bad seem pointless.

There was no denying this. Whatever it was that was happening between them, it was so compelling that Kit couldn't stop it.

She didn't want to stop it.

She languished in his embrace, relishing the feel of this man she'd been fighting an attraction to, finally giving in.

Slowly, gently, he lowered with her to the floor, the warmth of his arm beneath her a contrast to the cold of the carpet.

Cal kissed her with breathtaking skill, his tongue deft in drawing out her most intimate desire, his hands drawing her further under his spell without once making her stop and think better of what she was doing with him.

He pulled her closer to him, and Kit felt every nerve spring to attention, reveling in the strength and demand of his arms.

"Is this what you want?" he asked her, surprising her with his consideration.

She smiled. "How much more obvious can I make it?"

He laughed softly and lowered his mouth onto hers again.

He'd kissed her before, raising her curiosity and, yes, making her want him. But this time it was different.

This time it was more real.

And she knew, from the tingle of her spine to the molten heat of her insides, that she wouldn't be satisfied until he'd filled her completely.

It seemed it was the same for him. She pressed forward against him and felt his desire, hard and strong.

He cupped his hands to her face and said, "I want you more than I've ever wanted anyone before."

She hesitated for just a fraction of a second, and he captured her lips once again in silent persuasion.

"Me, too," she managed—just barely—to whisper.

She reached to the front of his pants, where his buckle had been pressing against her abdomen, and she pulled the leather loose, unhinging it and drawing the long strap out of his pants in a slow, tantalizing motion.

He let out a long breath and tangled his fingers in her hair, his breathing growing shallow as she proceeded to undo the button and pull his pants down, along with his briefs, over his slender hips.

She glanced into his eyes before taking the next step.

He drew his hand around to the back of her head and pulled her closer for a long, deep kiss.

As his tongue worked magic against her own, lowering whatever resistance she had left, he unbuttoned her pants in one deft move and slipped her pants down over her thighs.

Without a thought she kicked them off, eager to have him within her.

He touched his fingertips lightly against her thigh, teasing the skin into tickled gooseflesh, until he finally moved his fingers into the damp folds of her womanhood. She shifted her hips underneath his touch, moving almost against her intention, arching toward him as he brought her closer to ecstasy.

He lifted himself and settled over her, catching her mouth with his, communicating on a level much more meaningful than words could ever be. At last he thrust himself into her, meeting on the most primal level a man and woman can share.

And Kit smiled against his kiss, feeling a sensation so satisfying that she felt as if she was an empty pitcher being filled slowly with warm water.

The warmth filled her completely. It wasn't merely physical—it was emotional, too. Almost spiritual.

Was Cal just so skilled that she had never felt such exquisite physical pleasure before and it was fooling her into thinking it was more? Or *was* there something more to it?

For just a moment she tried to ponder the question, as if figuring out the answer was important. But as he moved against her, all thought was edged out until finally there was nothing left but a burst of pleasure and then…peace.

Afterward, as they lay in each other's arms, lightly touching fingertips to fingertips and skin to skin, Kit asked the question she shouldn't have.

"So what was it that happened between you and Breck Monahan?"

Cal looked down at her, idly trailing his hand across her skin. "You don't want to know."

"Yes, I do. I mean, really, how bad could it be?"

He nodded in the semidarkness. "It wasn't that bad."

She made an exasperated noise. "Then *tell me,* would you?"

He blew air into his cheeks, then out in one long hiss. "It was at the magazine's twenty-fifth anniversary party in June. I met this beautiful woman, started talking to her—like guys will do—and one thing led to another."

Kit's stomach clenched. "As in, you slept with her?"

"Well, yeah." His tone implied *Of course! What else would you expect?* .

And maybe she should expect that sort of thing. After all, he was a guy. But she didn't have one-night stands herself and she had sort of hoped that what had just happened between them meant more than that.

Now she couldn't be sure.

"Anyway," Cal went on, apparently unaware of the tension that had filled Kit's body, "the woman was Monahan's mistress, which I should have known because there was never, ever an attractive woman in the realm of *Sports World* before. She began to call me, trying to pursue a relationship. He found out about it and decided to screw us both, one way or another."

Kit suddenly hated this nameless, faceless woman who had caused so much damage. It wasn't fair, of course, Kit knew that, but it was still the truth. Blaming Cal was appropriate, too, but under the current circumstances, it was a little less comfortable.

"So now Monahan wants you to fail, seemingly on your own, so he can humiliate you without dragging himself into it."

"Right. Or his wife."

Kit added Monahan to her mental hate list. For a moment she even felt a surge of appreciation for

Rick, whose only crime as a husband was being too laid-back and unambitious. But then she thought about the way Cal's touch had felt on her—and in her—and she knew she hadn't made a mistake in leaving a marriage that didn't have that kind of passion.

Even though she couldn't say that sharing that passion with Cal wasn't a mistake.

It was all a mess.

"So that's pretty much it," Cal finished. He sat up and handed her her shirt. "Here. You seem chilly."

He didn't know the half of it. "Thanks." She put the shirt on and looked at him. "Tell me this," she said. "Have you had a lot of flings like that?"

"Flings?"

She shrugged. "One-night stands. Whatever you'd call them."

"Oh." He tipped a flattened palm from side to side. "It depends on your definition of *a lot*."

She groaned inwardly "That means yes."

He gave a half smile. "You might think so."

She swallowed her objection. After all, it was none of her business. He'd made no promises to her, and it wouldn't be fair for her to try and hold him to anything just because they'd had some tequila and succumbed to a mutual attraction.

It happened all the time.

Just not to her.

But maybe this was just one more way in which she was woefully out of touch with the real world. Maybe no matter what she did, she was always going to be an old-fashioned June Cleaver at heart.

Chapter Seventeen

Cal thought maybe it had been a mistake to tell Kit about his past. Not that he'd told her that much, but she was obviously upset by what she had heard, especially given what had happened between him and her.

He probably should also have told her that she was different. That what he felt for her was different.

The problem was, he was having trouble wrapping his mind around it himself. It was such classic Psychology 101 that he felt as if there had to be a catch.

The only women he'd ever been involved with were either timid, clinging vines—as his mother had been—who could bleed a man dry or sexy airheads who didn't want anything more than a hot night together and a predawn escape to the real world.

He'd spent most of his time recently with the latter. No demands, no expectations. They didn't give a lot, either, of course. At least, not outside the bedroom. But that was okay—he was willing to make that deal.

But Kit was different from all of that. She was so sexy it made his muscles ache just to look at her, probably from the effort of holding himself back. But she was smart, too. Generous with her time and her energy and her care.

She was an awesome mother to Johnny.

Even that was attractive, Cal thought.

Which left him with…what exactly? Was he infatuated? Would it pass? Or was this—he almost hated to entertain the idea—something deeper than that?

He hoped it wasn't, because he just wasn't equipped to deal with that kind of thing. Real relationships.

Love.

No, Cal Panagos had always been a loner and he wasn't going to change that now.

* * *

"Come on, Kit, he's a *guy*. You can't make assumptions about us—you have to just *ask*."

There were times when it was handy to have an ex-husband with whom Kit could speak freely about her mistakes in romance, and this was one of those times.

Rick had brought Johnny back late the next afternoon and they'd found Kit by the pool, trying to bake her worries away.

Johnny was already splashing away with his friends, and Rick was perched on the end of Kit's chaise lounge, telling her what she already knew but didn't want to admit.

She knew nothing about men.

"If you want to know how the guy feels about you, ask him," Rick said as if it were just that simple.

"But what if I don't like his answer?" Kit smiled. "And don't tell me to grow up and face the real world, because I'm not up for that right now."

Rick chuckled. "Far be it from me to tell you to grow up. But facing the real world might be good for you. Look, it sounds like you really like this guy. The fact that he's had one-night stands doesn't mean anything about how he does or doesn't feel about you. I've had one or two of them myself."

Kit was shocked. She never would have pegged Rick as a one-night-stand guy.

Then again, she wouldn't have pegged Jo as a one-night-stand girl, and Jo had set her straight on that.

So maybe it was Kit who was different. Maybe Kit was just out of touch. Maybe she was going to have to force herself to become a little more modern and a lot more open-minded.

"Mommy! Dad!" Johnny waved frantically from the side of the pool. "Watch this!" He jumped in, drawing his legs up slightly toward a cannonball position.

"Way to go!" Kit called.

"All *right!*" Rick ran over to him, high-fived him and came back to Kit. "Say what you want about our divorce, but I'll never be sorry we were married. That kid is the greatest."

"Yeah." Kit smiled, watching her son paddling around with his thick swim vest on.

"And so are you," Rick added, patting her leg. "You deserve the best. If you think that's this guy, then give it a chance."

She sighed. "I'll give it some thought."

"Hey, I almost forgot," Rick said. "I saw an ad for your premier issue in the local TV guide."

"You did?" She'd meant to look for that. Cal's promotions people were doing a big media blitz this week, starting today. "Did it intrigue you?"

"Of course. I've already bookmarked the site."

"Mmm." Kit smiled. "Too bad you don't have a computer."

Rick gave his goofy grin. "Okay, but I would have if I did have a computer." He stood up. "Got to go, babe. But think about what I said."

"I will."

"One more thing."

Kit looked up.

"I was hoping to take Johnny to a showing day after tomorrow over at the Lithuanian Hall in Kearny. They're going to introduce my mural plans. Got any problem with that?"

"Of course not," Kit said earnestly. "That'll be really cool for him. And for you—congratulations. Go by Brothers Bakery and have a few butter cookies for me, would you?"

"Sure thing." Rick bent down and gave her a quick kiss on top of the head. "Meanwhile, you take care of you."

"I will," she promised, then wondered just what in the world was the best way to do that while still keeping everyone else happy.

The truth was, Kit was very grateful for the fact that Rick wanted to spend more time with Johnny this week because she was going crazy with work.

Some days she was there until as late as eight or nine at night, working with Cal, Jo, Parker and a handful of support staff in order to put the new Web site together. Every time they thought they had it worked out perfectly, some new glitch would turn up and they'd have to solve it without causing a host of new problems.

By Monday night, though, it all seemed to be in perfect working order. The staff toasted the site with reasonably good French champagne—Cal said they'd have to save the Veuve Clicquot Ponsardin for a higher level of success—and everyone left in ones and twos, until Cal and Kit were, as usual, the last ones left.

"This is it," Cal said. "This week we find out if we sink or swim."

Kit drew in a tight breath. It was never far from her mind that she was supposed to close on her new house in three and a half weeks, and she had her loan officer's assurance that nothing was going to stop it this time.

"A friend told me he'd seen our ad in the local television guide," she said.

Cal nodded, considering. "That's just the tip of the iceberg. It's not even the tip. It's an ice cube. We've got an all-out blitz planned. It's a whole lot of money that could potentially go right down the drain if it doesn't work."

Kit sat down by his desk. "You're being too negative."

He looked at her. "I've burned every ounce of my life force on this project for more than a month now," he said. "Let me have just a minute or two to worry about the worst."

Kit laughed. "No. Not yet. We need positive thoughts and energy more than ever right now."

That got a smile out of him. "You're always difficult, aren't you?"

"Depends how you look at it."

He nodded. "Difficult. But cute. That's your saving grace. Or mine. I'm not sure which."

An unseen force pulsed between them. She wanted to question him, to find out why they hadn't talked about what had happened between them the other night, what it meant, if anything.

But she couldn't be the one to bring it up. There was too much danger of looking desperate and she didn't want him to view her that way. She'd find a way to talk to him about it, but not here and not now. And definitely not out of discomfort and needing a Band-Aid of empty promises on her bruised ego.

They sat in silence for a few seconds, then Cal looked out the window, then back at Kit. "You're here late. Is Johnny with your ex again?"

She nodded. "They had an art show to go to."

"Is Johnny interested in art already?" He looked surprised.

"Sort of. His dad's the artist, though, so he's interested in that. And Rick wanted to show him off, I think."

Cal gave a genuinely warm smile. "So…are you busy?"

"When?"

"Right now."

She reminded herself not to look too eager. "My only plans are to get some much-needed sleep."

He nodded, studying her. Then after a moment he said, "Think you could be persuaded to take a few minutes out of your schedule to go somewhere with me?"

"That depends," she said, sounding more coy than she'd meant to. "Where?"

Cal stood up. "It's a surprise."

She must have looked skeptical because he added, "A good one. You'll like it, I think."

She gave a skeptical frown. "Your surprises occasionally leave people out of work."

He shook his head when she would rather he vehemently denied it. "I can't make any guarantees, but this time if anyone's out of work, it's going to be me." He took her by the arm and started to escort her from his office. "So you see, I'm differently motivated this time. Trust me."

She stopped and looked at him. "Can I trust you, Cal? Really?" She didn't say how much she meant it, how deeply she cared to know, but he seemed to pick up on that.

After a moment's consideration he let out a short breath. "I'll never lie to you, Kit. You can trust me to be honest, no matter how ugly the truth might be. Apart from that, I can't make any promises. I've never been good at that."

It wasn't exactly the answer she'd been hoping for, but Kit had been around long enough to know there was a lot to be said for honesty. And so far his honesty hadn't broken her heart, so she'd go with it.

At least a little longer.

Chapter Eighteen

They stepped out into the balmy night just as a cab was approaching. Cal hailed it and ushered Kit inside.

"What are you up to?" she asked.

"You'll see." He leaned forward and told the driver to take them to Broadway and Forty-second. Then he leaned back against the seat next to Kit and turned to look at her. "Close your eyes."

A lot of childhood mishaps had begun that way. "I'm not closing my eyes, Cal."

He smiled, so charming even her feet felt hot. "Come on. It's just a few more blocks."

They were in the back of a smelly New York City cab, but suddenly Kit was remembering backseat limo love scenes from the movies and thinking thoughts about Cal that were better left unspoken. And unthought.

"I'm *not* closing my eyes," she said firmly, but she couldn't suppress a smile. "I'll get carsick."

"Suit yourself." He smiled and looked out the front window, giving her the opportunity to admire his straight, masculine profile. It really was quite nice.

She smiled to herself, thinking of her first impression of him. How angry she'd felt at his smooth delivery of bad news about the fate of *Home Life,* yet how struck she'd been by his good looks.

Little had she known how completely her opinion of the man was going to turn around.

Now she looked at his mouth, and instead of her initial detached observation of the grim line as he'd delivered the news, she remembered kissing his lips, feeling them all over her body, feeling him within her most private reaches.

She felt warm with remembering.

"Everything okay?" he asked.

"What?" she asked, a little startled. "Yes, fine. Why?"

"You suddenly looked a little squirmy."

"I'm fine." Good lord, if she wasn't careful, she was going to end up acting out her thoughts. And that would be very bad.

The cab turned a corner and Times Square lit up before them. The car was suddenly illuminated almost as light as day.

Kit turned a querulous look at Cal and he said, "We've got another block to go. We couldn't afford to go *this* far." The cab rounded another corner and Cal instructed him to stop. He handed the driver a bill and guided Kit out of the car.

He put his arms on her shoulders and turned her. "Ready?" he asked, his voice low and soft near her ear.

A shiver ran down her spine. She was ready, all right. She'd been ready for days. She nodded. "I guess so."

He turned her and said, "Look up."

She did. And there before her was a large billboard that simply said *DiaryofaDomesticGoddess.com—Read it and win.*

Kit gasped. "Are you kidding?" Her eyes played over the words again. The name of her column, there, as large as life in the heart of the city.

"That would be an expensive joke."

"But—my column?"

He nodded. "It's good. It's real good. And more

than that, it's the identity of the magazine now. I'm banking on your opinion."

Kit swallowed. No one had ever had so much faith in her. Ever since she was little, her mother had second-guessed—and often overridden—every decision she'd made. It wasn't as if she suffered for the sins of her mother still, but it had set a precedent of emotional hurdles and obstacles blocking the way to good self-esteem.

It wasn't until she'd had Johnny, actually, and watched him thrive under her care that she'd begun to think she might really be good at something.

But this? This was a vote of confidence she hadn't been counting on.

Her eyes burned with unshed tears and there was a lump so hard in her throat she could barely speak. "I can't believe this."

Cal looked concerned. "Do you like it?"

She sniffed and nodded, managing a smile. "Of course I like it. I *love* it. I'm not at all sure anything I've done merits this. In fact, I'm pretty sure it hasn't."

"Don't sell yourself short." He put his arm around her shoulder and drew her into the warmth of his body.

She leaned against him, glad for the steady strength of his embrace because without it she thought she might have turned to a rag doll.

"You may be surprised to hear it, given our rocky start, but I've got a lot of faith in you," Cal said to her.

His words thrilled her, filled her, yet she clung to an impulse to hide how much it meant to her. "Well, you certainly kept that well hidden for a while."

He shrugged. "I didn't want you to get a big head."

"Yeah, right."

"Seriously, Kit, you should be damn proud of yourself. I am. You fought for what you believed was best for the magazine and our demographic and you convinced me." He gave that sly pirate smile. "And if you can convince *me,* it should be no sweat convincing the rest of the world."

She swallowed hard. "You're crazy."

He looked into her eyes. "I think I'm getting that way."

Their gaze held for a long time before he slowly lowered his mouth onto hers and kissed her gently but deeply.

The crowd of people around them receded until Kit had no awareness of anything but Cal and the beat of her own heart. She could have stayed there forever, kissing him, and she would have been happy with that.

"How about coming back to my place?" he asked her. "It's not far."

She nodded mutely.

Somehow Cal managed to hail a cab right away and they climbed into the car like a couple of eager teenagers. Cal gave the address, then turned and kissed Kit again.

But she was *not* going to simulate one of those love scenes in the back of a public cab, so she drew back. "Easy there," she said. "We keep going like that and we're not going to be able to stop."

"That's the idea." He moved toward her again.

She smiled and put her hands up in front of her, pressing against his chest as he came in for the kiss. "Not here."

"You're killing me," he groaned and leaned back against the dingy seat. "But you're right."

"So…what do people win if they go to my site?"

"A hundred grand."

She blinked. "I'm sorry?"

"A hundred thousand dollars."

"But—but *how?*"

He gave half a shrug. "Advertising budget. Don't forget we saved a bundle by not going to press."

"I know, but still—that's a lot of money."

He nodded. "I know. When the promotions people first mentioned it, I was a little nervous myself, but they suggested an essay contest based on your column. Sort of a 'write your own mini Domestic

Goddess column and win.' The contest runs all month, and they've designed it so people can come back and check if they've won smaller prizes every day. We get more hits, more word of mouth, more advance subscriptions and everyone wins."

"I hope you know what you're doing."

The look he gave her was different than the one he'd just been wearing. This wasn't desire or sensuality, it was quiet, businesslike confidence. "I know what I'm doing, Kit. Trust me. You do your thing, I'll do mine."

For the first time in years Kit felt herself relax and give up control. When Cal said he had things in hand, she believed him, and the freedom she felt was incredible.

The cab drew to a stop in front of a luxury apartment and Kit and Cal got out. She barely registered the walk through the highly polished lobby or the smooth ride up to the penthouse. All she could think about, all she could see, was Cal Panagos.

When they got to his apartment, they were so completely unable to keep their hands off each other that they practically tumbled in the door together.

He kicked the door shut and they didn't say a word—they just began pulling each other's clothes off.

When he pulled her against his bare chest, she felt

like a watercolor paint bleeding onto paper. She almost felt as if she was part of him.

"Think we can make it to the bedroom this time?" he asked between kisses.

"Yes," she murmured, intoxicated by the taste and the feel of him. Her gaze lowered to his mouth, and she felt a surge of adrenaline driving her toward him. "But we'd better hurry."

He rose and swiftly lifted her into his arms. It was like something from a corny old movie, but it wasn't corny and it was definitely real. He carried her through the dimly lit hallway into a darkened bedroom, kissing her all along the way, until finally he laid her down on the soft surface of his bed.

The room was dark, but the lights of the city twinkled outside, providing enough light for Kit to see and appreciate the contours of Cal's well-formed body.

She couldn't wait to have him inside of her again.

She pulled him toward her and kissed him deeply. Their tongues sought each other and met, intensifying the pounding of her heart and drawing their bodies even closer, until it seemed there was no space whatsoever between them. Just one long seam of passion.

He braced his hands on her lower back and rolled over, taking her with him. Then he ran his fingertips back and forth over the bare skin of her back, artfully making her arch closer into him.

He ran his hands around the sensitive skin of her ribs, and cupped them around her breasts. "You are incredible," he whispered.

She straddled him, so ready for his passion it was all she could do to move carefully.

As he entered her, they rolled over again so that he was on top, commanding her movements. She crossed her ankles behind his lower back and drew him into her.

He smiled. "We're getting good at this." He moved, catching her desire.

She drew in a sharp breath. "Practice makes perfect."

"I'm willing to keep working at it if you are." He pulled back a little and then pushed in again, deeper.

Kit felt as if he filled her, as if his body and his soul had melded completely with hers.

They moved together like a machine, no awkwardness, no mistakes. His movements were easy at first, slowly building a fire inside Kit's core that would soon turn to an inferno. She knew he felt the same because his movements quickened at the exact pace she needed them to. No words were spoken, yet volumes were expressed.

Faster and faster they moved together until Kit felt the explosion of sensation fill her. Then the long, steady drift downward, like a feather pleasantly dancing along the wind, until she sighed her final shudder of satisfaction.

It was unlike anything she'd ever felt before.

Cal twined his fingers with Kit's and kissed her again. "I don't want you to go home."

"Johnny's not going to come back until tomorrow."

"I don't just mean now. I mean ever. I want to just stay here with you forever."

She smiled. "That would negate all of our hard work."

"Ah, so what? We can always build a new empire."

She laughed. "Spoken like a true winner."

He looked at her. She could see his face, half shaded and half lit by the light from outside. "It's hard not to feel like a winner with you on my team, Kit. I mean that."

She was so touched she couldn't speak. Instead she just squeezed his hand.

"But I guess you're right," he went on. "We've worked pretty hard, we may as well see what comes of it. At the office, I mean," he amended quickly.

She laughed.

"This is the week, Kit. This week we find out where we stand."

Neither one of them knew just how true that was.

Chapter Nineteen

The magazine was a hit.

As a matter of fact, it was what one could characterize as an *instant* hit.

The Sissy Searles case Max Trilling was covering had taken an explosive turn when another former child star, long rumored to be dead, came forward as a witness. Trilling—at his best under pressure—had managed to cover the revelation on time to be the first personal account of it published.

The response to the other articles was also very positive. Cal and Kit had chosen well, filling the site with incisive, fascinating pieces, each of which pushed the envelope of their various genres just a little bit, taking them beyond the ordinary.

With Jo's encouragement and cheerleading, Kit had revised her own article on the Passion Princess party, adding detail she hadn't included in the first version. It had segued neatly into the question of dating as a single parent, and Jo had assured Kit the end product was laugh-out-loud funny in addition to being titillating and relevant to their target audience. Although Kit had second, third and fourth thoughts—many of which involved the negative reaction she anticipated from her mother and certain churchgoing friends and relatives—Kit let Parker put it on the site and resisted the subsequent urge to make him pull it.

The response from readers was overwhelming.

As the weeks passed, Cal came alive with the challenge of dealing with success, and his PR team jumped on the idea of promoting Kit as a personality as well as the author of the column.

The whole notion struck her as silly, but she agreed to do a couple of local television appearances, and afterward Parker reported a hundredfold increase in site hits.

After several weeks of this circus of promotion and publicity, Kit had already had enough. But it looked as if the magazine was going to stay in business—at least long enough for her to get her house and keep drawing a salary long enough to hold on to it for a while.

Plus, every column she wrote was something she could proudly put on her résumé to help ensure continued job security.

The first print issue was scheduled for September and would hit the stands within the week, Kit's house closing was two days away and all felt right with her world when Cal dropped the bomb.

"I'm leaving the magazine," he said to her.

It was a gorgeous late-summer evening and they were cooking out in the grassy patch behind her apartment building while Johnny played with a couple of his friends on the tot lot in front of them.

It was the first couple-ish thing they'd done together; the first time she'd had Cal over with Johnny around.

And apparently it was the last time, too.

Kit felt as though she'd been punched in the stomach. "You're what?" She looked at him incredulously. He had to be kidding. Didn't he? Why would he leave already? It had only just barely become a success. Things were still very, very tenuous. "You're joking, right?"

He shook his head and smiled as Johnny sailed down the sliding board on his stomach. "I got an offer I couldn't refuse. For a new publication that's starting up in California. They heard about our success and contacted me a couple of weeks ago."

"California!" Across the country! Thousands of miles away! Didn't they have something together? Had she just made a stupid assumption about where things stood between them when, in fact, Cal had been looking at it as a casual fling? "And you've known this for a couple of weeks but you didn't say anything?" How many times had they made love in that time, growing closer and closer—or so Kit thought—all the while Cal knowing he wasn't going to be around much longer.

Had he even thought about what it meant to leave their relationship? Worse, was that what had taken those two weeks? Had he weighed the relative merits of their newly budding relationship versus a trip across the country and decided he'd rather take the chance on the new job?

"I don't have a choice, Kit," Cal said, looking at her earnestly. "You know as well as I do that Monahan could still turn on me if I was working for him. There was no way I could sit here and wait for him to ambush me. But don't worry, your job is safe. He's bringing in Tony Fueselli, and Tony's a great guy. You'll like working with him."

She wasn't thinking about her job for the moment. Visions of tanned, thin, blond California girls danced tauntingly in her head. Visions of Cal *with* those tanned, thin, blond California girls made her stomach twist in a knot.

"California is so far away."

"I have to go where the work is."

"But…" A thousand objections lodged in her throat, but they all came down to *What about me?* And she didn't want to be the kind of woman who said that. "You're needed here."

He shook his head and looked at his hands—or the ground or anything but Kit. "At this point, I'm not bringing anything to the magazine that any other qualified person couldn't."

"I didn't mean at the magazine," she said, and her voice went weak with the words. Emotion filled her and she fastened her eyes on Johnny, laughing and playing in the distance, so she didn't look at Cal and let him see the depth of her emotion.

"What did you mean—" He stopped and she felt his hand on her arm. "Oh. You mean… I'm sorry, Kit, I misunderstood. Look, you and I can still see each other."

His voice was so impersonal, as if it was an afterthought. Kit hated herself for persisting, but she couldn't help it.

"Really?" she asked. "How? California moved, you know—it's not just down the street anymore."

He sighed. "I know it's far away, but we can get together. Maybe meet halfway."

She did look at him now, challenging him with the anger that came of realizing he was scraping her off and he wasn't even being very graceful about it. "You know I have obligations here that would prevent me from weekend tête-à-têtes in Chicago or Nevada or San Diego or whatever you'd consider *meeting halfway*. But thanks for the offer." She stood up. "I think you'd better go."

He looked sad but not surprised. "Kit, come on." He stood and put his hands on her shoulders. "Please try to understand."

"I think I do," she said, looking him squarely in the eye. She didn't care if he saw the heartbreak and disappointment there. What did she have to lose? She'd already lost the most important part of her. "I think I understand all too well."

He didn't argue.

God, she wanted him to. She wanted him to say something—anything—to reassure her that he cared about her and he wanted to be with her and that he'd try to make it work somehow.

At this point she'd almost settle for a bad lie.

But that wasn't Cal's style. It never had been.

"I'm sorry," he said softly.

And though he'd never lied to her before—at least not that she knew of—she didn't believe he was sorry.

He certainly didn't look it.

Which meant there was no good reason for her to stick around and let him break her heart further. The only thing that could happen if they prolonged this conversation was that she could actually end up crying and begging and making a complete fool of herself.

She might have lost the guy but she was at least determined to hold on to her dignity.

"Goodbye, Cal," she said curtly so he couldn't hear the waver in her voice. She got up and focused her attention on the playground.

"Kit—"

She ignored him. "Johnny!" she called, walking away from Cal and toward the only being with testosterone she knew she could believe in. "Let's go, buddy."

"Go where?" Johnny asked, running toward her.

"Inside." She hoped he didn't sense her upset. "I'll put some spaghetti on."

Johnny looked puzzled. "But Cal's making hamburgers." He glanced behind Kit. "He's right there." He gestured toward the man she knew was looking at them from several yards away.

She swallowed. "We've changed our plans," she said. "Cal has something else he has to do, so why don't you go say goodbye to him and we'll go in and have your favorite spaghetti, okay?"

Johnny frowned. "The stuff in the can?"

She hated to serve it to him, but she did keep it on hand for emergencies.

This felt as if it qualified.

She waited, watching from a short distance as Johnny ran over to Cal and high-fived him. They shared some sort of little joke, both of them laughed, then Johnny came running back over to her.

"He said he'll make the hamburgers for me another time," he said to her.

And for the first time since she'd met him Kit knew Cal had told a lie.

Cal replayed that moment in his head over and over again during the plane ride west. He had six hours to dwell on thoughts of Kit, and after four hours he realized he'd thought of little else.

Of course, it had been a week since he'd seen her, and she'd been on his mind plenty in that time, too. But the finality of boarding the plane and leaving New York was the thing that tipped his thoughts over the edge.

No matter where he looked, he saw something

that reminded him of Kit or of Johnny. He was surprised how much he missed the kid. They hadn't spent that much time together, but Cal had enjoyed it a lot and had been looking forward to spending more time with him. He'd even thought about maybe taking him to a Mets game or two.

That was off now, of course.

But it was on Cal's mind. There was a little blond-headed boy two aisles up who looked so much like Johnny that Cal had found himself doing double takes more than once.

Yet Cal knew there was no point in feeling bad about his decision. It had been the right thing. Hadn't it? He really hadn't had much of a choice.

Had he?

Yes, the job offer from California had been intriguing, and there was no doubt whatsoever that Breck Monahan would have found a way to stick it to him. But now that it was just him and himself on the plane, Cal had to admit he wasn't just doing this because of work.

He was doing it because of Kit.

This was best for her. She needed stability, especially because of Johnny. She didn't need a guy who'd never had a truly solid relationship. A guy, in fact, who'd never cared so much about a woman that he was willing to give anything up for her.

Of course, it could be argued that he was doing that now, giving up the best sex of his life in order to spare Kit the disappointment he would inevitably cause one day.

When he'd started work at what was then *Home Life,* he'd gotten a kick out of the spunky Kit and her logic-defying confidence in herself. At first he'd wanted to keep her around just to see what she'd have the nerve to come up with next.

And she'd never disappointed him. Every time he'd thought he had her figured out, she'd come out with something new and surprising that he wouldn't have expected of her.

But he'd taken things too far when he'd gotten romantically involved with her. After being absolutely up front with her about where he stood at work, he'd made the classic mistake of letting her believe he was emotionally available when he wasn't.

He looked out the window.

Or maybe his mistake had been in letting *himself* believe he was emotionally available. That he was willing to try.

Because he wasn't. No way. He had other, more pressing things to worry about. Like his livelihood. No one was giving him a free ride. He had to concentrate on survival first—there was no room in that equation for worrying about a woman.

Or obsessing about her. Thinking about her touch or her kiss when he was supposed to be working.

That was *not* for him.

Cal looked out the window at the clouds, like snowy mountains, below. He was nowhere. Over the earth, over the clouds—this was a feeling he normally loved.

Now he had a new normal.

A ball thumped across the floor and rolled under his seat, followed immediately by the boy he'd noticed earlier.

"Jake!" his mother snapped.

"I dropped my ball," the child explained to her, approaching Cal despite his mother's objections.

The mother got up and came over, giving Cal an apologetic smile. "I must have fallen asleep for a minute and he got away. Sorry to bother you."

"It's no bother." He reached under the seat and helped the boy find his ball. "Here you go," he said, handing it to him.

The little fingers grazed his hand and he felt sadness land in the pit of his stomach.

"Thanks!" the boy said. "What's your name?"

His mother looked embarrassed and grasped his upper arm. "Come *on,* Jake."

Cal held up a hand. "It's okay, really. My name's Cal," he told the boy. "And you're Jake."

The boy's brown eyes opened wide. "How'd you know?"

Cal laughed. "Because that's what your mom just called you. How old are you, Jake? Four?"

Now Jake's eyes were wide with amazement. "How'd you know *that?*"

"Lucky guess."

"Wow." Jake went back to his seat looking as if he'd just seen a magician.

When had Cal become the kind of guy who knew how old kids were?

About a month ago, he realized. When Kit and Johnny had come into his life and, damn it, into his heart.

He closed his eyes and leaned back against the seat. He never should have allowed himself to feel anything for Kit. This move had come at exactly the right time. One more month and he probably would have been married, for Pete's sake.

God knew Cal Panagos was not the marrying kind.

And he was *definitely* not the stepdad kind.

No doubt about it, he'd gotten out just in time.

"Can I give you a ride home?"

"No, thanks." Kit frantically searched the street for a cab so she could get away from this catastrophe of a date.

Saturday afternoon in New York City and not a cab to be found!

"I'd be happy to walk you there."

To New Jersey? She feigned a cough and tried to make it sound frighteningly contagious. "You know, I'm just not feeling that well. I'd hate to get you sick." Where were all the cabs? Why was it Cal had been able to flag one down the very minute he thought of it, but when she needed one the streets were empty.

Not even a bicycle courier zoomed by, and at this point she would have paid a primo price for his handlebars.

"Kat—"

"Kit." Why was she correcting him? Was she crazy? If he had her name wrong, more power to him. "Kitty, actually," she heard herself say. This was getting more ridiculous by the moment.

Eventually, when she was finally in the safety of a closed and locked taxi, this would probably seem funny. Or at least it would be good fodder for her column.

"I'd really like to spend more time with you."

She coughed again. "You know, I'm just not feeling up to it right now. I think I'd better go home and get some rest."

He wasn't buying it. "This isn't because I'm a janitor, is it?"

Kit stopped and looked at the six-foot-four man before her, taking in the blond Marilyn Monroe wig, the pink spaghetti-strap dress, the high wedge heels and the large gold hoop earrings with cubic zirconia stars dangling in the middle. "No, Mario. It's not because you're a janitor."

Things had reached a new low.

"It's Mari*a*, actually."

And *another* new low.

Kit sighed. "Yet your profile on makemea-match.com said Mari*o*, so perhaps you can imagine my surprise when we met." She looked down the street again. Nothing. Maybe if she got to a busier road she'd have better luck. She began to walk and he followed, clopping along behind her in his clunky Jimmy Choo knock-offs. "To be honest, I really just don't see this working out," she said. "We're not each other's type."

"Wait a minute, this isn't because…" He laughed as if the idea was almost too preposterous to entertain. "Is this because I'm a transvestite?"

Kit stopped and looked him dead in the eye. "That's a big part of it, yes."

Mario shook his head spastically. "I am so *sick* of this kind of ignorance. I am *not* gay, I simply like to wear this style of clothing. If you can't accept that, then the hell with you."

She smiled. "Okay, then. We're agreed. But Mario—you might want to mention this in your on-line profile. I'm guessing it will save you a lot of time."

At last—at *last*—a taxi came trundling down the street. Kit stepped into the street to hail it, putting herself dangerously close to its path so it would *have* to stop.

Mercifully it did.

"It was nice meeting you," she lied to the angry-looking man in the pink dress. "Good luck!" To the driver she said, "Just go, fast, before he follows us."

The driver gunned the engine and drove away, turning a block up when Kit told him the address for her home. She didn't care that she had to take the cab all the way to New Jersey. After the day she'd had, she was willing to pay double just to get home and forget the whole dating idea.

She had packing to do. That would be a lot more fun. As would patching the holes in the wall and painting.

Frankly shoving bamboo shoots under her own fingernails would have been more fun at this point.

It was all Cal Panagos's fault. He'd been gone three and a half weeks now and she had moped around so long that even Johnny had begun looking at her a little nervously. So Kit had decided the only way to get over Cal was to get out there and start meeting new people.

And she had succeeded, in the sense that she'd wanted to meet someone very different from Cal. But after this, she was starting to think she'd really much rather be alone.

If only she could stop thinking about Cal.

Since her lunch date had ended early, she arrived home in the early afternoon and faced the whole day and night with nothing to do. Johnny was with Rick, and Jo and Parker had gone upstate to camp.

It was probably just as well, Kit thought. She was closing on the house in a week and there was still packing to do. It's just that the packing wasn't doing much to keep her mind off her loneliness.

She missed Cal.

She worked through the afternoon, putting things in boxes and then writing down notes for her column on dating. It was going to be hard to avoid writing details that would make Mario recognizable, but the story was just too good to not use.

It was early evening, and Kit had just finished a toaster pastry for dinner when the door buzzer buzzed.

She leaped to her feet to answer it, glad for any interruption at this point.

When she opened the door, she couldn't believe her eyes. Cal stood there, weary-eyed, with a suitcase in hand. "I hear this apartment is about to be vacant," he said.

Kit's heart was so filled she couldn't speak for a moment. "I believe if you want to rent it, you have to go through the rental office," she said, studying his face. But she couldn't joke for long. "Cal, what are you doing here?"

He set the suitcase down, freeing the strong, square hands she'd grown to love. "Getting ready to beg for the first time in my life," he told her.

She swallowed the lump of emotion that was forcing its way into her throat. "Beg for what?"

"Forgiveness. Mercy." He stepped forward and touched his hand to her cheek. "You."

"Me?" she breathed.

He nodded. "Can you ever forgive me for being stupid enough to give up what we had?"

At the moment her heart sang *yes*, but she knew she had to be more cautious. Her heart had gotten her into trouble with Cal before. "What exactly are you asking?"

"That you let me come in and make up for lost time."

She couldn't let herself dare to hope. She couldn't assume anything. "Are you just here for the weekend?"

He looked at her squarely and shook his head.

"No, Kit. I'm here for good." He let out a long breath. "Look, I was stupid. There's no other way to put it. I was so afraid of getting close that I was willing to walk away."

She had to be careful, even though she wanted to throw herself into his arms. "What changed your mind?"

He smiled and shook his head. "A little boy on the plane."

It wasn't an answer she'd been expecting. "What?"

"It was a lot of things," he said. "I missed you. I missed Johnny. What used to be life to me felt empty without you."

Her heart thrummed in her chest. She wanted to believe this. She wanted it more than anything. "What about your job?"

"I told them I had to do it from here or I couldn't do it at all."

She blinked. "And?"

He gave a half shrug. "I've applied at the gas station down the road here."

She smiled and shook her head. "Liar."

"You're right. I'm working from here."

She felt as if she was conducting a job interview. "And where is *here?*"

"*Here* is as close as I can get to you," he said in a quietly husky voice. "And if you won't let it be *here*—" he stepped directly in front of her and took her into his arms "—then I'll just keep trying until you let me."

She looked up into his face. "Better try hard," she said with a sly smile.

He smiled back and it took her breath away. "I intend to." He kissed her, cupping his hands to her face as if she was something delicate and precious. "Every day for the rest of my life. So what would you say to a new merger?"

She'd say yes and she knew it. She'd known it the moment she'd seen him standing on her doorstep. "Well, I don't know. I'm not sure we can work that well together."

"Sure we can. We've done it before."

She raised an eyebrow. "This isn't a buyout in disguise?"

He crossed a finger over his heart. "Nope. A fifty-fifty partnership."

"I don't want to share the profits if it's only short-term."

"No way. I'm in it for the long haul." He kissed her. "So what do you say?"

She smiled and stepped back. "I say, come in, Mr. Panagos. We've got some heavy-duty negotiating to do."

* * * * *

SPECIAL EDITION™

presents a new continuity

FAMILY BUSINESS

Bound by fate, members of a shattered family
renew their ties—and find a legacy of love.

On sale January 2006

PRODIGAL SON

by award-winning author

Susan Mallery

After his father's death, eldest son Jack Hanson
reluctantly assumed responsibility for the family
media business. But when the company faced
dire straits, Jack was forced to depend on
himself—and the skills of the one woman he
promised long ago he'd never fall for....

Don't miss this compelling story—only from
Silhouette Books.

Available at your favorite retail outlet.

Silhouette®

COMING NEXT MONTH

#1729 PRODIGAL SON—Susan Mallery
Family Business
After his father's death, it was up to eldest son Jack Hanson to save the troubled family business. Hiring his beautiful business school rival Samantha Edwards helped—her creative ideas worked wonders. But her unorthodox style rankled by-the-books Jack. They were headed for an office showdown...*and* falling for each other behind closed doors.

#1730 A PERFECT LIFE—Patricia Kay
Callie's Corner Café
The divorce was tough enough on Shawn Fletcher—selling the house and watching her ex remarry *really* stung. So a flirtation with her daughter's math teacher, Matt McFarland, came as a nice surprise. But when things with the younger man seemed serious, Shawn panicked—how would her daughter and the Callie's Corner Café gang take the news?

#1731 HIS MOTHER'S WEDDING—Judy Duarte
Private eye Rico Garcia blamed his cynicism about romance on his mom, who after four marriages had found a "soul mate"—again! Rico's help with the new wedding put him on a collision course with gorgeous, Pollyanna-ish wedding planner Molly Townsend. The attraction sizzled...but was it enough to melt the detective's world-weary veneer?

#1732 HIS COMFORT AND JOY—Jessica Bird
The Moorehouse Legacy
For dress designer Joy Moorehouse, July and August were the kindest months—when brash politico Gray Bennett summered in her hometown of Saranac. She innocently admired him from afar until things between them took a sudden turn. Soon work led Joy to Gray's Manhattan stomping ground...and passions escalated in a New York minute.

#1733 THE THREE-WAY MIRACLE—Karen Sandler
Devoted to managing the Rescued Hearts Riding School, Sara Rand kept men at arm's length, and volunteer building contractor Keith Delacroix was no exception. But then Sara and Keith had to join forces to find a missing student. Looking for the little girl made them reflect on loss and abuse in their pasts, and mutual attraction in the present....

#1734 THE DOCTOR'S SECRET CHILD—Kate Welsh
CEO Caroline Hopewell knew heartbreak. Her father had died, leaving her to raise his son by a second marriage, and the boy had a rare illness. Then Caroline discovered the truth: the child wasn't her father's. But the endearing attentions of the true dad, Dr. Trey Westerly, for his newfound child stirred Caroline's soul... giving her hope for the future.